She laughed again

and began to run her fingers across his chest, combing his hair with her nails. Clint trembled, yet even he could not say if it was due to sensual pleasure or fear. Fear? The Gunsmith never would have believed he could be so unnerved by an unarmed woman, yet he'd never encountered one even remotely similar to Sylvia Jarrad.

"You're not afraid of me, are you, Clint?" she said, her hands sliding along his stomach.

"Should I be?" he replied.

Don't miss any of the lusty, hard-riding action in the new Charter
Western series, THE GUNSMITH:

And coming next month:

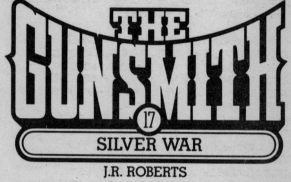

THE GUNSMITH

17
SILVER WAR

J.R. ROBERTS

CHARTER BOOKS, NEW YORK

THE GUNSMITH #17: SILVER WAR

A Charter Book/published by arrangement with
the author

PRINTING HISTORY
Charter edition/June 1983

ISBN: 0-441-30887-2

Charter Books are published by Charter Communications, Inc.
200 Madison Avenue, New York, N.Y. 10016.
PRINTED IN THE UNITED STATES OF AMERICA

To Rena Wolner,
with sincere thanks.

J.R. ROBERTS

ONE

Nevada had a lot to offer . . . if a man knew where to look for it. Although most of the state is located in the desert region of the Great Basin, Nevada has tremendous natural resources, providing one is willing to exert enough effort to get to them. The desert doesn't surrender anything easily. Farmers could grow crops along the Humboldt Sink if they dug into the earth to tap the underground streams for irrigation. Ranchers raised large herds of cattle, but only after they went to extra trouble to supply the animals with food and water in an environment that provided little of either. Silver, copper and gold deposits offered great wealth to anyone willing to break his back mining for them. It was all there, if you wanted it badly enough to work for it.

Clint Adams wasn't a farmer, rancher or miner, but he'd been attracted to Nevada for reasons of personal profit as well. Clint was a businessman, the sole owner and operator of a traveling gunsmith shop. Wherever there were men in the West, there were guns. Towns were springing up in Nevada, and Clint naturally favored those that promised the greatest demand for his services.

He knew he'd never get rich with his little traveling business, but Clint wasn't interested in becoming wealthy. He'd met enough people who valued gold more than lives and money more than happiness. Not that Clint Adams was a particularly happy man, but he was satisfied with who and what he was, which is more than most men can claim.

Who was Clint Adams? A tall, leanly muscled man who'd managed to remain fit and healthy although he'd seen more than forty summers. His features were pleasant and quietly handsome. Only the scar on his left cheek suggested he was familiar with violence.

He'd worn a badge for years, but he'd become disillusioned with the life of a lawman and, to a degree, with people in general and their attitudes about the law in particular.

And: Clint Adams was the Gunsmith, whether he liked it or not—and most of the time, he didn't care for the moniker at all. Being a "living legend" had proven to be a burden and Clint imagined that one day his fame would get him killed. A snot-nosed kid looking for a reputation might one day pull the trigger, but that damn newspaper man who'd first stuck the name "The Gunsmith" on him had started the music for his funeral dirge years ago.

Death wasn't something Clint worried about. Few things really concerned the Gunsmith as he traveled throughout the West in his wagon which contained all his worldly possessions. Tied to the rear of his rig was the magnificent black Arabian gelding Duke, who had been with the Gunsmith since the animal was a mere colt. Clint regarded Duke as more than just a horse. He was Clint's friend, companion and colleague on the trail.

"Our trip's been going pretty well so far, hasn't it, big fella?" Clint called back to Duke.

The gelding neighed and bobbed his head in reply, perhaps merely responding to Clint's voice or perhaps, as the Gunsmith believed, the horse truly understood his words.

"Yeah," Clint grinned. "So far we haven't gotten into any trouble this time."

He'd rolled his wagon across the border from California, thus avoiding the formidable deserts of the Yucca and Alkali Flats. He'd visited Carson City for a while and made a nice profit fixing and modifying firearms for the residents. Then he'd moved on to Silver City and enjoyed a couple of mildly prosperous days' business before heading south for the Silver Peak Range.

Clint had decided to make his journey into Nevada in autumn in order to avoid the stifling heat of the desert in the summer or the bitterly cold nights during the winter. The weather that fall was remarkably pleasant. A cool breeze from the north eased the normally hot, dry climate of the Great Basin.

The Gunsmith traveled near the California-Nevada border, favoring the prairies to the deserts. The area was remarkably flat and the sandy ground was solid enough to make travel by wagon easy. Although barren and somber, the terrain had a strange, haunting beauty. Occasional rock formations dotted the landscape like macabre sculptures. In the distance, the gray humps of hills and boulders lurked at the fringes of the brilliant blue horizon.

The environment didn't frighten Clint despite its harsh appearance. He noticed patches of sagebrush and buffalo grass jutting from the cracked bed of an arroyo, which suggested an underground stream. This was confirmed when Clint saw a pair of small pronghorn antelope descend into the arroyo to paw the ground with their sharp hooves and lap at the muddy liquid beneath the surface.

Occasionally, Clint spotted a lizard sunning itself on a rock. Once he noticed a large snake stretched across a flat stone, its forked tongue slithering lazily in and out between its jaws. Clint couldn't see it well enough to determine if it was a rattler or just a big bull snake. Clint even got a glimpse of a desert bighorn sheep which stood at the summit of a butte. A well-muscled ram with great curved horns, the animal seemed to watch the Gunsmith's wagon with suspicion as the rig made its way across the prairie.

As Clint approached a cluster of rock formations, he noticed a set of wheel tracks on the ground between the wide gap in the center. Drawing closer to the pass, he saw another vehicle positioned near one of the rock walls. He didn't see anyone in the driver's seat and wondered if the wagon had rolled into a ditch or broken an axle. It was an Eastern-style buggy with a canvas roof and a single horse harnessed to the rig. *Hell of a contraption to ride around in out in the middle of the Great Basin. . . .*

Then he saw two or three figures thrashing about on the ground near the buggy. The confused cluster of arms and legs made it difficult to determine how many were involved in the wrestling match, but he saw buckskin-clad arms that appeared to be masculine and a couple of long legs encased in dark stockings that were undoubtedly feminine. The legs kicked wildly, exposing white petticoats. A girl's cry for help mingled with men's drunken laughter. The Gunsmith had just stumbled upon a rape in progress.

Clint slapped the reins across the backs of his team horses to urge them into a gallop.

A figure suddenly materialized in front of Clint. Dressed in buckskin shirt and breeches, the man's dark, copper-brown face was framed by shoulder-length black hair with two eagle feathers jutting from a headband. Probably a Shoshoni, Clint thought, not that it made any difference what tribe the Indian belonged to. The Henry carbine in the man's hands was all that concerned Clint at the moment.

The Indian threw the buttstock of his weapon to his shoulder and aimed the Henry at Clint's chest. The Gunsmith leaned to the left, his right hand diving for the pistol on his hip while the other remained fisted around the reins.

Although the Shoshoni's finger was on the trigger of his carbine and he had caught Clint off guard, he spent a shred of a second too long aiming. The Gunsmith's Colt cleared leather and roared before the brave could squeeze the trigger. The impact of a .45 slug through the forehead sent the Indian flying backward to fall heavily on the hard ground. The Shoshoni's carbine was still in his fists, held in a frozen death grip.

Clint yanked back on the reins to bring the team to a halt, his wagon less than twenty feet from the buggy. Two more Shoshoni rose up from the struggling forms by the side of the road. Each fierce-faced brave held a six-gun and tried to draw a bead on Clint.

If the Gunsmith had been armed with a single-action revolver, he would have been dead, but his modified double-action Colt allowed him to fire more rapidly than his opponents who had to cock their weapons before they could shoot. Clint squeezed off two shots, the explosions rolling quickly together to sound like one long blast.

Shooting double-action isn't as accurate as single-action, but at such close range the Gunsmith had no trouble putting a bullet squarely in each man's chest. One still struggled to sit up, his gun still in his fist. Clint's pistol snarled and the Shoshoni's face exploded.

Clint glanced about to be certain he'd dealt with the last aggressor, then he approached the figure lying near the rocks—and she proved to have quite a figure indeed.

The front of the woman's dress had been ripped open revealing a generous view of cleavage. Her breasts were still encased in a chemise, but they were obviously large and firm like two ripe melons. Her skirt was bunched up around her waist, the long shapely legs and petticoats fully exposed.

The girl stared up at Clint, her dark brown eyes wide with astonishment. Rich, full lips formed an oval as she nodded her head in mute thanks, still too stunned to speak. Then, she suddenly pulled down her skirt and grabbed the front of her dress, trying to hold it together.

"Are you all right?" the Gunsmith inquired, holstering his pistol. He offered a hand to the girl.

She took it and Clint hauled her to her feet. She brushed a few strands of long dark brown hair from her face and tried to get a mental grip on herself.

"Uh—yes. Thank you, sir." Her voice revealed a New England background. "It appears you saved me from a fate worse than death, as they say."

"Not really," Clint replied dryly. "After they'd all had a turn with you, they would have killed you, ma'am."

TWO

"Are you always so blunt, Mr.—?" the girl asked stiffly.

"Adams," the Gunsmith replied. "Clint Adams, at your service, ma'am."

"You've already been quite a service, Mr. Adams."

"I'd rather be called Clint by a pretty lady," he grinned.

She smiled in response, the expression lighting up her face. "Such flattery. Good with a gun and just as good with words. That interests me because words are my profession."

"Oh?" Clint raised his eyebrows slightly. The girl had recovered quickly from her ordeal and he detected an authoritative attitude about her.

"I'm Darlene Farrell of *The Boston Weekly*," she declared, thrusting out her right hand while the left held her dress together.

"Uh-huh," Clint shook her hand. "You're a newspaper . . . woman?"

"Do I detect a certain animosity?" she asked slyly. "I take it you don't approve of women reporters?"

"I approve of women"—Clint smiled—"but I've never been overly fond of journalists in general."

7

"Oh?" She sniffed with indignation. "And what do you have against people in my profession?"

"Too many of them tend to bend the truth to sell more papers," Clint replied flatly. "They exaggerate and distort facts in order to make a story more colorful. Sometimes those distortions hurt somebody, but damn few newspaper men seem to care about that."

"What about newspaperwomen?" Darlene inquired, taking the criticism in stride, probably because she couldn't deny the truth in Clint's remarks.

"I haven't known that many of them to form a general opinion," he replied.

"Or a prejudice?"

"Not really much difference is there?" the Gunsmith mused. "One just sounds a bit more polite than the other. However, if it makes you feel better, one of the few people in your profession I've known whom I liked and respected was a woman who ran a newspaper in Avalon, New Mexico."

"I hope I can live up to her qualifications," Darlene commented dryly.

One of the reasons Clint had liked J.T. Archer was because she'd been beautiful and great in bed. Darlene was certainly as lovely and Clint wondered if she'd be as good in the other category as the lady editor had been.

"Are you traveling out here alone, Darlene?" Clint asked.

"Well, yes," the girl replied as she headed for her buggy. "I certainly didn't expect to have any trouble from the Indians. I was told they were pretty tame in this state."

"Indians are people," the Gunsmith said. "Some good, some bad. You find outlaws, bandits and renegades everywhere in every country, culture, race and level of society."

Darlene turned to face Clint, an expression of curiosity on her lovely features. "You seem to be a rather philosophical man for a cowboy, Clint."

"I'm not a cowboy," he grinned. "I'm a traveling . . . salesman."

Clint had almost admitted he was a gunsmith, but he decided to remain vague about his profession since Darlene was a newspaperwoman. She obviously hadn't recognized his name, but Darlene had seen him handle a gun and she might guess he was the Gunsmith if he told her how he made a living. The last thing Clint wanted was another reporter trying to get a story at his expense. Every time somebody in the press contributed to the legend of the Gunsmith it meant more trouble for Clint Adams.

"Oh," Darlene seemed disappointed. "What do you sell?"

"Goods and services," Clint replied. "I'm a small businessman trying to make the most of the free enterprise system."

"You certainly know how to use that gun."

"That's something a lot of men learn to do," Clint said. "It makes sense if you want to survive. Speaking of which, do you have a gun?"

"Me?" She seemed stunned by the question. "Good Heavens, no! I've never handled a gun in my life. . . ."

"If you plan to be riding around out here by yourself you'd better learn," Clint advised. "Where are you headed anyway?"

"Lodeville," she replied.

"Well, I'm headed in that direction. I'll sort of tag along with you just in case you have any more trouble. Okay?"

"I'd really appreciate that, Clint," she told him. "I had hoped to put together an exciting story for my newspaper, but I hadn't expected to get personally involved.''

"Really?" Clint smiled. "Then why'd you come out here?"

Her eyes flashed at the remark. *Pretty women always look magnificent when they're angry,* Clint thought.

"I'm here to get first-hand information," Darlene replied sharply. "So I can write accurate *facts,* not distortions or exaggerations—the very things you criticize journalists for doing!"

"Very commendable." Clint nodded. "Any particular story you're interested in?"

"Well"—she seemed to cool down, aware that her temper was getting the better of her—"silver seems to be doing for Nevada what the gold rush did for California. People are flocking to the state. Towns are being constructed and businesses are booming out here. I want to do a story on what the Nevada of the future will be like. When the mad rush for silver is over, what will happen to the people who remain here?"

"Sounds good," Clint said. "Quite provocative, but I'd steer clear of the mining towns if I were you. They can be pretty rough."

"You sound like my editor." Darlene sighed. "He didn't think a woman should come out here alone either."

"He probably had your best interests in mind."

"I can take care of myself—"

Clint canted his head toward the three dead Shoshoni braves.

"Well," Darlene cleared her throat in an embarrassed manner. "If we're going to Lodeville, don't you think we should be on our way?"

THREE

The tiny caravan of Darlene's buggy and Clint's gunsmith wagon traveled the rest of the afternoon without incident. Clint noticed the sun was slowly heading toward some jagged peaks in the western horizon. The air had already begun to cool while the sky adopted a darker shade of blue and the clouds seemed to soften at their centers as a golden halo surrounded their cottonlike forms.

"Darlene," Clint called to the buggy.

The girl pulled on the reins of her one-horse carriage to bring it to a halt. She looked back at Clint's wagon to see it had also stopped.

"Is something wrong, Clint?" she inquired, watching him climb down from his vehicle.

"Not really," he assured her as he approached the buggy. "I think God knew what He was doing when He decided to have day and night. You might notice the latter is going to occur in another hour or two."

Darlene looked up at the sky and frowned. "I thought we would have reached Lodeville by now."

Clint shook his head. "That's at least fifty miles from here."

Her eyes expanded with surprise. "Fifty miles? That can't be right. I have a map that an old prospector made for me in Silver City. He'd told me Lodeville was only sixty

11

miles away and I'm certain I've covered more than twenty since I left—''

"Darlene," Clint began, "I left Silver City a few days ago and it's almost forty miles from where we are now."

The girl was stunned. "But the prospector—"

"Is probably illiterate and used to judging distance by the sun and various landmarks," Clint explained. "I'm certain the oldtimer could find his way to Lodeville easily enough, but he probably hasn't used a map for years. Prospectors who make enough trips out here begin to misjudge the distance, either exaggerating or understating the number of miles. You happened to get one of the former."

"And how can you be certain you're right and my map is wrong?" Darlene demanded.

"Because my maps were made by a geographical surveyor who measured the area for the United States government when they were trying to decide the locations for cavalry posts back in 1867."

"Oh," Darlene replied, unable to dispute the probable accuracy of Clint's source of information. "Well, we can still try to cover another mile or two before dark."

"I have to advise against that, Darlene," he stated. "You see, nightfall can be sort of sudden out here. Sometimes twilight just falls like a curtain. One minute it's dusk and the next you're looking up at a skyfull of stars."

"It did seem to get dark rather suddenly last night," she admitted. "So you're suggesting we make our camp now?"

Clint nodded. "That way we'll have time to get everything set up without fumbling around in the dark."

"Well, I imagine you're more experienced in these matters than I am," she agreed, climbing down from her buggy. "You've been to Nevada before, Clint?"

"Yeah," he replied. "I was here a while back for a poker tournament in a place called Two Queens—"

He stopped before his tongue could become too careless. The newspaper woman hadn't recognized his name and Clint wanted to keep it that way. During the poker tournament at Two Queens there had been a series of bizarre murders which Clint had investigated and eventually solved.

"A poker tournament?" she raised an eyebrow. "I thought you were a salesman, not a gambler."

"I'm a professional salesman," Clint smiled. "But I'm still fond of poker."

"You mean you're lucky?"

"No man who plays poker well relies on luck."

"Then you claim poker is a game of skill instead of mere chance." She smiled. "That's a rather old debate, isn't it?"

"Yeah," Clint agreed. "Folks who consistently lose at poker like to think of it as just luck—usually bad. The rest of us know that it requires a good deal of skill to be good at poker. You have to know the game and the odds of success with whatever hand you've been dealt. You have to know what your chances are of getting a better hand before you discard and when to fold on a weak hand or try to bluff your way through."

"I suppose bluffing can be a skill in itself."

"At times," Clint agreed. "Although I don't care to rely on it unless I have to."

"You certainly don't have to bluff when it comes to using a gun. . . ."

"We'd better pitch camp, Darlene," Clint advised, wanting to steer the conversation away from his prowess with a pistol. "Unhitch your horse and I'll give her a rubdown after we feed and water her."

"You noticed my horse is a mare?" Darlene raised an eyebrow.

Clint shrugged. "A man has to know horse flesh out here. You've got a Morgan-mustang cross-breed from the looks of her. Lots of stamina but not much speed. Still a good choice for a carriage horse."

"I'm impressed, Clint," she smiled. "Is there anything you don't know?"

"I don't know if you intend to cook dinner tonight or take a chance on my ability instead."

Darlene laughed. "You take care of the horses and leave the preparation of dinner to me."

"Sounds like a fair deal," Clint agreed. "I'll gather up some sagebrush and greasewood for the fire before I take care of Duke and the animals."

"Duke?" she wrinkled her brow.

"He's hitched to the back of my rig. The most beautiful Arabian gelding you'll ever see."

"Why did you say 'Duke *and* the animals'?"

"Force of habit."

By the time they'd completed the chores necessary to set up camp, twilight had fallen. The sky adopted a deep velvet color and a majestic array of stars and a quarter-moon appeared overhead. Clint covered the horses with blankets and brushed Duke's glossy black coat, petting the gelding and talking to him as though he was a person before he draped Duke's personal hand-woven Navajo blanket over his back and neck.

Darlene had packed a rather small supply of salt pork, beans and a couple loaves of ready-baked bread that had already begun to go stale. Although the meal was better than most Clint ate on the trail, he advised her that canned sardines, tomatoes, sourdough bread and jerky were better suited for travel in the West.

"Once again, I'm indebted to you for your advice, Clint," Darlene replied as they sat by the campfire, drinking coffee from tin cups.

"My pleasure," he replied, noticing how lovely she was in the flickering light of the campfire. It seemed to caress her features with the soft glow of candlelight. "But in the future you might do well to try to prepare a little better before embarking on any adventures—especially alone."

"Well," she began, rising from her blanket to approach the Gunsmith. "I'm not alone right now."

"Until we get to a town," he nodded. His pulse quickened as the girl knelt on his bedroll next to him. "I guess we've got each other."

"Then we've both got our careers to consider," Darlene commented, placing her cup on one of the stones that surrounded the fire. "I've got my journalism and you've got—whatever it is you do."

"Oh," Clint began, putting down his cup as well. "I do a lot of things."

"And do them all well?" Darlene inquired, moving closer.

"I don't get too many complaints," he admitted, snaking an arm around her waist.

Darlene responded by wrapping her arms around his neck and their mouths quickly met in a fiery, passionate kiss. Tongues sought the caverns of each other's mouths as their hands slowly caressed and explored. Fingers fumbled with buttons and buckles even as they sprawled full-length across the Gunsmith's bedroll.

"It got pretty chilly last night," Darlene commented, reaching back to unfasten her dress.

"Reckon we'll both be warm enough tonight," Clint assured her as he unbuckled his gunbelt and hung it on the horn of his saddle which sat at the head of his bedroll.

Clint removed his shirt and trousers while he watched Darlene strip. The glow of the campfire flickered across her bare shoulders and the tops of her breasts as the dress fell at her feet. Next she unbuttoned her silk chemise and slid it down the shapely curves of her body.

Darlene's naked breasts bobbed proudly, the nipples erect and firm. Clint smiled approvingly at her flat belly, rounded hips, long smooth thighs and well-shaped legs. Clint felt his manhood strain against the fabric of his long johns as he eagerly began to peel off his underwear.

The girl grinned too as she drew closer. Darlene helped him pull down his long johns and knelt before Clint. Her soft lips brushed against his stiff member, the tongue licking his shaft like a friendly puppy. Darlene's fingers reached between his legs and cupped his testicles in her palm as her lips parted to accept his maleness. Clint felt the fire in his loins build as she drew deeply on his penis, kissing and sucking as though gathering nourishment from his erection.

Her head slowly began to move to and fro, her warm, damp mouth stroking his penis. The tempo gradually increased and Clint felt his load build rapidly. Then Darlene stopped and withdrew her mouth from his hard organ. Clint lowered himself to the blanket and she was upon him, nearly throwing the Gunsmith off balance by the force of her lunge.

Clint found himself on his back almost before he realized what had happened. Darlene quickly straddled his crotch, seizing his manhood to hastily guide it into the dark, damp cavern between her thighs.

Darlene's knees clamped against Clint's hips as she began to squirm against his groin, grinding his penis deeper inside her tunnel of love. Clint's hands found her breasts and he gently thumbed her erect nipples, marveling at their hardness. He braced himself on one hand and managed to sit up enough to kiss her breasts. He tongued them passionately, teasing the stiff nipples with his teeth.

Then the strain on his arm became too great and Clint collapsed on his back, surrendering to the attention Darlene had devoted to his manhood. She began to rock back and forth and gradually rose up and down, riding the length of his shaft like a child on a rocking horse. Yet she wasn't a child; Darlene made love like a woman of considerable experience and skill.

Not that this disturbed the Gunsmith. Clint wasn't a hypocrite about sex. If a man improved with experience, the same naturally held true for a woman, and Darlene certainly knew how to attend to a man's needs.

Clint had never been a selfish lover. He bucked his loins and arched his back to thrust himself deeper into the girl, trying to contribute to her fulfillment as well as his own. Her groans of pleasure assured him of success. The girl's nails raked his chest and her groans turned into a wail of ecstasy when an orgasm shuddered through her.

She sat astride him, breathing hard, eyes closed and hair strewn wildly about her shoulders and face, yet Clint saw the contented grin on her luscious mouth. Darlene didn't move, still savoring his hardness within her. Slowly, she combed back her hair and looked down at him.

"I can see why you haven't gotten many complaints," Darlene remarked.

Then she rode his manhood again. This time she nearly went into a frenzy and once bounced clear of his erect shaft. Darlene muttered "shit" and hastily inserted his member again to continue her wild lovemaking. When she reached the limit, her nails clawed into his chest, but he barely noticed as he released his seed at the same moment and was too preoccupied with pleasure to notice such mild pain. Again, Darlene cried out from paradise.

As though in reply, a coyote howled somewhere in prairie beyond.

FOUR

It seemed like just about everything in Nevada had been named after silver—Silver Peak, Silver Point, Silver City—so it came as no surprise to encounter a sign that bore the legend SILVERTOWN, *Population 358*.

Clint wondered how many other Silvertowns and Silvervilles were scattered throughout the state. No one could fault the founders of any mining community for naming it after the precious metal that offered wealth and prosperity to those who'd labored so hard to acquire it. To Clint Adams, however, it would have made more sense to name a place Minerstown or Minerville after the men who'd broken their backs for long months to get the silver out of the ground. Blood and Sweat or Determination would have been even more appropriate. The Gunsmith admired richness of character more than material wealth. Anyone who could get the formidable terrain of the Great Basin to yield anything deserved recognition for the accomplishment.

Darlene's buggy and Clint's wagon entered the community of Silvertown in the midmorning. The town was filled with people swarming about the streets, mostly merchants and shop owners preparing to receive customers at noon. A few townsfolk stared at Darlene's horse and buggy, which looked as out of place in a mining town as a

19

lace doily on a Longhorn steer. Otherwise no one paid much attention to the newcomers. People were always shuffling in and out of places like Silvertown.

Discovering the town had been a surprise to the Gunsmith as well as Darlene since it hadn't been on either of their maps. They'd been heading for Lodeville in the Excelsior Mountains when they practically stumbled upon Silvertown.

Clint had seen such towns before. The typical mining town consisted of only a few solid structures, most dwellings being little more than canvas tents or tarps with poles hastily jammed together to serve as a giant lean-to. Silvertown was put together better than most. It contained dozens of buildings and most were constructed of the most dependable and durable substance available in a desert—adobe. This seemed to suggest Silvertown was meant to be more or less permanent. Obviously, many of the residents planned to remain after the silver mines petered out.

There was no doubt, however, that the town had been made to service miners. Clint counted three general stores and five saloons. Painted-faced whores gazed down from windows overlooking the batwings and displayed professional smiles when they saw the Gunsmith.

Darlene spotted a telegraph office and stopped her rig in front of the building. She climbed down from the buggy and hurried inside the office, forgetting to tie the reins of her horse to the hitching-rail in her haste. Clint brought his wagon to a halt behind the buggy and climbed down, shaking his head at the girl's carelessness. In a mining town, a drunk or angry resident might start shooting at the drop of a hat so it's always best to secure a horse unless you don't mind if it bolts to the next county.

Of course, Clint's team had been trained to overcome gunshyness, so he figured it was safe to leave them for a couple minutes—long enough to tie Darlene's mare to the rail and to go inside the office and tell her he was going to see to Duke and his rig. The girl was busy sending a telegram to her editor in Boston and absentmindedly nodded in reply.

"Fine, Clint," she said without looking at him. "Fine."

Silvertown had a livery stable and a corral which specialized in selling mules and donkeys to miners. A few pathetic old veterans of the mines were segregated from the younger, healthy animals. The mules were scrawny beasts with dull coats and pale muzzles. Blind from spending days in the dark, damp caverns and nights exposed to the elements, the poor animals bunched together as if trying to find some comfort while they waited for the merciful executions that would take them from misery to the glue pot.

Clint headed for the livery stable and asked a rather bored young hostler how much he'd charge to look after the wagon and horses. The youth yawned and scratched the blond peach-fuzz under his jaw.

"Pretty fair amount of space you'll be takin' up with all them critters and that rig," the hostler remarked. "Gonna have to charge you 'bout two dollars a day for all that—includin' food and water for the hosses, of course."

Clint fished out his billfold. "I'll pay you five dollars a day to make sure you give my wagon and horses extra-special care."

"Oh!" the hostler's eyes widened. "Well, sure, mister."

"But you listen up, friend," Clint said sternly. "I want you to earn this money. That wagon had better be secure and left unmolested. My team horses had better be fed, watered and brushed down. And, I want you to treat that big black gelding like he belonged to the President of the United States."

"Yes, sir." The kid nodded eagerly.

"I'll be back to check on how you've taken care of everything. If I'm happy with your work, I'll pay you a nice bonus. Otherwise, you're going to wish your Pa had thought your Ma was too ugly to go to bed with. Understand?"

The youth gulped nervously. "Don't worry none, Mr.—"

"Adams," the Gunsmith replied. "Clint Adams."

"Clint Adams?" the hostler's mouth fell open. "You mean you're the Gunsmith?"

"You take care of my valuables. Okay, boy?"

The kid nodded so hard Clint was afraid he might work his neck loose. The Gunsmith strolled out of the livery stable. *Maybe, once in a while, it helps to be famous*, he thought.

Maybe . . .

FIVE

Darlene's horse and buggy were no longer parked in front of the telegraph office. Clint considered looking for her, but decided not to work at it. He and the lady journalist would have to part company sooner or later and he'd rather do it before she discovered who he was.

Following a custom of courtesy to the local law, he headed for the sheriff's office. A weary man with a potbelly and a dense brown beard streaked with gray sat in a rocking chair behind a small, ill-treated desk. The star-shaped badge pinned to his checkered shirt identified him as the sheriff. Clint heard the lawman snore as he entered the office.

"Sheriff?" he asked, just to be sure.

"Huh?" the old man muttered. He raised his head and gazed at his visitor through sleep-fogged eyes. "What you want, feller?"

"I'm Clint Adams."

"You a new miner in town or somethin'?" the sheriff asked with a yawn.

Maybe I'm not as famous as I figured, Clint thought. "No, Sheriff. I'm just a stranger in town and I stopped by to let you know I'll probably be here for a while, trying to drum up some business. I'm a traveling gunsmith. Do repairs and modifications of firearms for a living."

"Oh," the lawman nodded. "Fine, son. Just don't start no trouble."

"I don't aim to, sir," Clint assured him. "Thanks for your time."

Clint turned to leave.

"Gunsmith!" the sheriff exclaimed, the information suddenly sinking into his dull brain. "You mean you're *the* Gunsmith?"

"I didn't say that, Sheriff," Clint replied mildly. "But that's what some folks call me. See you later."

Clint Adams liked saloons. Taverns are the best places in the world to find relaxed, talkative men in a group. Most patrons in saloons are in a good mood—surly or depressed drunks being the obvious exceptions to this rule—and quite a few tend to be careless with their money and easily talked into doing business with a fellow who offers them a good deal.

By two in the afternoon, Clint had visited every saloon in Silvertown. Half a dozen miners, a few shop owners and two bartenders told him they had firearms in need of repair and agreed that Clint's prices sounded reasonable. The prospective customers promised to get in touch with him either that evening or the next day. Clint left the last saloon, feeling pretty good about the unexpected opportunity for profit in the tiny community of Silvertown.

"Clint Adams?" a deep, masculine voice inquired as the Gunsmith stepped onto the plankwalk outside the saloon.

"Yeah?" Clint replied, turning to face the speaker.

He was surprised to see a husky man dressed in pinstriped suit trousers and a matching vest. A black derby perched on his dark blond head contributed to his eastern appearance. The man wore a wide leather belt with brass studs decorating its entire length, but no holstered pistol hung on his hip.

Still, no one would mistake the fellow for a drummer—even if one failed to notice the leather strap of a shoulder holster at the edge of his vest or the bulge of a revolver butt under his left arm. The man's face was broad and hard and his blue green eyes resembled colored stones jammed into the sockets behind hooded lids. Maybe the fellow came from back East, but he wasn't a greenhorn salesman or tourist. *Hardcase* was written on him from the top of his derby to the heels of his hobnail boots.

"I've heard a good deal about you, Adams," he declared. "Even back in Baltimore we've heard tales about the Gunsmith."

"Somehow," Clint began, "I don't think you're interested in my autograph."

The easterner smiled with all the warmth of a crack in a tombstone. "I'm working for a man named Alfred W. Jarrad. He's got a cattle ranch located near the Silver Peak Mountains. He'd be real pleased to make your acquaintance."

"As a matter of fact, I plan to head that way in a couple days." Clint shrugged. "Maybe I'll see your employer then."

"Why wait?" the man asked. "I'm going back to the ranch today. You can follow me and meet with Mr. Jarrad in time for supper. He sets a mighty fine table and he can be a real good host."

"I've got business here in Silvertown," Clint explained.

"You can have business at the Big J spread too, Adams," the easterner told him. "Jarrad needs a man like you. He'll pay you one thousand dollars a month, plus bonuses for extra services."

"I'm a gunsmith," Clint declared. "Not a gunman."

"Way I hear it, you're good with a gun. You're also an ex-lawman and you know the country. You know how crooked bastards think out here."

"Crooked bastards think about the same everywhere," Clint commented.

"But they don't always act the same," the stranger insisted. "The Big J has been having trouble with cattle rustlers. Me, I'm from the city. I know how to handle the scum on the streets and what alleys and dives to look into when the sons of bitches bolt. I don't do so good out here on the range where the outlaws ride horses and play hide and seek among rocks and arroyos."

"What's your name, friend?" Clint asked. "You an ex-policeman?"

The man smiled thinly. "I'm called Baltimore Smith. I wasn't a policeman exactly. I used to work for a detective agency."

"Pinkerton?"

"Smaller than Pinkerton," Smith replied. "But we've done some work together from time to time. Old Alan P. hired a couple of us to help investigate the Molly Maguires. They're sort of a secret society of Irish fanatics that popped up among the coal miners in Pennsylvania about ten years ago and they've been burning, bashing, killing and blowing up things ever since."

"I've heard of them," Clint assured him. "How'd your investigation turn out?"

"The Mollies killed both my partners." Smith shrugged. "So I came out here looking for a new place to start over."

"Running down rustlers is a big change from being a detective back East," Clint commented.

"Maybe, but I figure scum is scum. You're from the

East, Adams, and you seem to have learned to handle yourself pretty well out here. I'll learn too.''

Smith pulled a turnip-shaped watch from a vest pocket. "I'm going to leave soon, Adams. You want to come along with me to the Big J or not?''

Clint had considered the offer. Trading lead with cow thieves wasn't the sort of job he'd usually accept, but a thousand dollars was a lot more than he could hope to make repairing firearms in Silvertown. The job seemed legal enough and more or less respectable.

Also, it presented an opportunity to get out of town before Darlene could learn he was the Gunsmith and thus avoid being hounded by the newslady, who had no doubt already put together a thrilling story about how Clint Adams had rescued her from the Shoshoni. If she told many people about the incident, she'd certainly learn about the Gunsmith.

"Let me get my wagon,'' Clint told Smith.

SIX

The Big J Ranch was quite a place. The spread consisted of thousands of acres of grazing land that was remarkably fertile for the Great Basin. Clint was stunned to see miles of tall, healthy grass and hundreds of plump, well-fed cattle. Barbed wire fencing surrounded the property and keen-eyed, sharp-faced men were stationed near the wire. More than one sentry swung a Winchester at the Gunsmith's wagon before Baltimore Smith curtly identified himself. The guards would then lower their rifles and nod, yet they still watched Clint's rig with unfettered suspicion.

The man from Maryland rode alongside Clint's wagon. The Gunsmith noticed that his guide rode a quarter horse with a McClellan saddle with ease. Baltimore Smith wasn't an inexperienced city slicker. Clint wondered how long his companion had been in Nevada and on Jarrad's payroll.

"Your boss seems to have pretty good security already," Clint told Smith, glancing at the sentries behind the wire.

"Not enough," Smith replied. "Jarrad will tell you why."

"How big is this spread?" Clint asked, gazing at the

28

long columns of barbed wire and fence posts that extended as far as the eye could see.

"We'll arrive in time for supper, Adams," Smith assured him. "Don't worry."

Indeed, the sun had begun to set and the sky assumed the soft shades of dusk before they reached the front gate. Three heavily armed guards greeted Baltimore Smith and opened the gate for them. Clint wondered what would have happened if he'd driven the wagon to the ranch without Smith beside him.

They rode along a wide, well-designed road that extended from the gate to the ranch house. Clint had expected Jarrad's house to be large and fancy, perhaps made of whitewashed adobe with Spanish-style roofing of red tile or modeled in the manner of an old southern plantation.

Alfred Jarrad's home was as startling as it was impressive. Three stories high with multicolored glass windows and a slope-peaked gray tile roof, it looked more like a European cathedral than a Nevada ranch house. The Gothic-style dwelling appeared to be made of red house bricks and the pillars supporting the porch roof looked like white marble.

"The house is sort of a shock at first, huh?" Smith commented.

"Does Jarrad plan to build a moat and drawbridge for the place in the future?" Clint inquired.

"Don't give him any ideas." Smith sounded serious. "There's a stable around back. You'll find a lot of other things there too—a blacksmith shop, barn for dairy cows, bunkhouses for the men and even a cantina to relax in after chores are done."

Clint whistled with admiration. "Is this a ranch or Jarrad's personal town?"

"Haven't quite figured that out yet myself," Smith said. "Right now, you just see to your horses and wagon. I'll tell the old man who you are and there'll be a place set for you at his dinner table, so be sure to wash up."

Although Clint had been told about the community-style arrangement, the sight still amazed him. Almost a dozen buildings of wood and adobe formed a great horse-shoe formation at the rear of the mansion. Signs identified several structures as a livery, cantina, laundry and one was simply labeled SHOP. The barn and bunkhouses were obvious and required no signs. The latter resembled a row of small army billets.

A white-haired Negro hostler met him at the stable and helped the Gunsmith with the wagon and animals. The black man stared at Duke as if he'd just laid eyes on paradise with four legs.

"That's purely one beautiful hoss, suh," the hostler remarked with sincere admiration.

"His name is Duke," the Gunsmith explained. "And you can call me Clint."

"That hoss is royalty, sure 'nough," the old man said, stroking Duke's neck as tenderly as most men would a woman's thigh. He turned to Clint, almost forgetting the human owner of the magnificent Arabian gelding. "Oh, my name is George, suh."

"Well, George," Clint smiled. "I think I can trust you to take care of Duke, but here's a dollar for your trouble."

"A dollar?" George stared at the silver eagle in Clint's hand. "What would I do with it, suh?"

The Gunsmith noticed George had chosen to disregard his invitation to address him by his first name. "You deserve to be paid for your work, George. . . ."

"Oh, I be paid." The hostler smiled. "Ain't like the old days when I was a slave in South Carolina. Always had a way with animals so I've been workin' in stables mosta my life. Got me a wife who works for Mr. Jarrad in the kitchen, and my children is being raised here too. Got me my family and a roof over our heads and plenty to eat. Besides, I get thirty dollars a month and I can come or go if'n I wants. So you just keep your money, suh. I'll be right pleased to see to the Duke here.''

"Have it your way, George." There was no point debating the issue with old George, Clint realized. He wondered whether Alfred W. Jarrad intended to put his brand on all his employees as he had with the old hostler.

Well, Clint thought, *if that's the way Jarrad wants to run his ranch, he can forget about hiring me to help him with some rustlers. If I don't like the set up, I can always ride on.*

But for now, he was hungry after a long ride and curious about what sort of man could turn barren prairies into pastures and build a mansion and a private town which he guarded as though it contained the national treasury.

SEVEN

Twenty minutes later, Clint Adams met the object of his
curiosity. Alfred Jarrad was a big man, with broad shoulders and a thick chest. His middle was also large, but it
seemed solid rather than flabby. Jarrad's torso resembled
a keg of nails—a comparison that fit the toughness of the
man.

His hands were large with square-tipped fingers and
scarred knuckles. Jarrad's broad face was tanned and
scored with lines by exposure to the elements. A mane of
silver hair framed his hard features and a great mustache,
shaped like the horns of a Texas steer, decorated his firm
mouth. The wire-rimmed glasses perched on the bridge of
his doorknob nose seemed alien to that face and the
gun-metal gray eyes that were magnified by the thick
lenses.

Baltimore Smith introduced Clint to the rancher when
Jarrad met them at the front door. Jarrad shook Clint's
hand, his grip firm and strong as he pumped the
Gunsmith's arm once in a no-nonsense manner.

"You've got quite a reputation, Adams," the rancher
remarked. "Baltimore figures you'd be a valuable asset to
us."

"That depends on what you expect me to do," Clint

replied. "Seems to me you've already got a lot of men on your payroll to guard your cattle, Mr. Jarrad."

"Let's talk about this over dinner," the rancher suggested as he turned to lead the way inside the mansion.

Clint and Baltimore Smith followed Jarrad through a long hallway with a checkerboard floor of red and yellow tile and a large staircase with polished wooden rails and red-carpeted steps.

The dining room was enormous with a large walnut table and leather-backed chairs. To Clint's surprise, he noticed a beatiful young girl seated at the chair to the left of the head of the table.

Her shoulder-length hair was a very pale and fine blond, almost the color of platinum. The girl's features were classically beautiful with a small nose, full mouth and large, remarkably dark blue eyes which inspected the Gunsmith with frank interest.

"Clint Adams," Jarrad began gruff introductions. "This is my daughter, Sylvia. Adams is a new man on my team, Sylvia."

"That's not quite official yet, Mr. Jarrad," Clint remarked.

"Be seated," the rancher instructed.

Jarrad sat at the head of the table while Baltimore Smith took a chair to his right. A plate, silverware, napkin and glasses were set in front of the chair beside Smith so Clint guessed this was where he was supposed to sit. A heavy-set black woman began placing trays of roast beef, baked bread, boiled potatoes and corn on the cob on the table.

"All right," Jarrad began as the maid poured red wine into glasses. "You got a good look at my spread on your way here. What did you notice, Adams?"

"Ranching isn't my forte," Clint admitted. "But you seem to have quite a few miles of excellent grazing land

and large herds of fit cattle—not to mention dozens of men to protect them.''

''You must figure I'm pretty lucky to have all that fine land, don't you?'' Jarrad's eyes hardened behind the thick lenses of his glasses. He wasn't asking a question as much as he was demanding a response.

Clint shook his head. ''No, sir. I know Nevada well enough to realize it isn't lucky for anyone. A man has to work to get anything out of this territory.''

''You're goddamn right I had to work for it!'' Jarrad declared fiercely. ''Dug down into underground streams and pumped the water up to irrigate the fields. Had to dam up a river north of here at the Silver Peak Range in order to reroute it and keep a steady supply of water for my land and cattle. That's why my property is the best in the state and my beef is better than any you'll find west of Idaho.''

He thrust a steak knife at the roast beef in the center of the table. ''Taste it for yourself, Adams. It's the best, because I sweated blood to make certain it would be.''

''And since you've got the best,'' Clint began, ''you want to keep it?''

''Damn right I do,'' Jarrad confirmed. ''No rustlers, who are too lazy to work like I did, are going to take what's mine.''

''Don't you have a lot of men to protect your cattle from thieves?'' Clint inquired, taking Jarrad's suggestion and helping himself to the roast beef.

''A lot of people want what's mine,'' the rancher replied flatly. ''And not just the cattle. They want my land as well—the richest land in Nevada.''

''And you're paying a thousand dollars a man to guard it?'' Clint whistled softly.

''Most of the men you saw standing guard will receive considerably less than that,'' Jarrad answered. ''Most of them get two hundred a month, which is still damn good money. Men like you, Baltimore and Parako are worth five times as much as any one of them so you'll be paid accordingly.''

"Parako?" Clint frowned. "The same Parako who took Johnny Murdock in a gunfight a few months ago?"

"That's the one," Baltimore Smith confirmed. "Murdock was supposed to be pretty fast, but he wasn't fast enough.''

"He'd also retired a couple years before," the Gunsmith added. "He was running a chicken farm near Bridgeport before Parako found him.''

"Have you retired, Adams?" Jarrad inquired.

"I was a lawman," Clint explained. "I never was a gunman and never intend to be. Most of the time I make my living as a gunsmith, although occasionally I'll work at something else for a while.''

"Do you agree that a man has a right to protect what rightfully belongs to him?" Jarrad demanded. "What he struggled and scraped and sacrificed for? Don't you believe in that, Adams?''

"Yes, I do," Clint nodded. He glanced at Sylvia who still watched him with her deep midnight blue eyes, yet she hadn't said a word all evening. "And cattle rustlers aren't the sort of people I look upon with favor. Still, I can't say in advance how long I'll care to work at this sort of thing. . . .''

"A thousand a month, Adams," the rancher told him. "That's pretty good pay and if you don't like working for me—" He shrugged. "This property is fenced in and guarded to keep unwanted folks out, not to keep anyone from leaving. You can go any time you please, Adams.''

"Sounds fair," Clint agreed. "You've got yourself a new employee, Mr. Jarrad . . . at least, for a while.''

Again, Clint glanced at Sylvia. She smiled and nodded in mute approval of his decision.

EIGHT

After dinner, Clint left the house and strolled back to the livery stable to check on Duke and his gear, though there seemed little doubt that old George, the hostler, would take good care of the Gunsmith's property. He entered the stable, holding a coal-oil lantern in his left hand. No sooner had he closed the door than he heard soft, deep-throated laughter from somewhere among the shadows that filled the stable. Clint's right hand fell to the butt of his holstered revolver.

"Too late, Gunsmith," a man's voice rasped. "If I'd wanted you dead, I would have shot you already. Made a fine target, coming in here with that lantern lit up pretty. Must be getting careless in your old age, huh?"

"Maybe," Clint replied, trying to locate the speaker. The man's voice seemed vaguely familiar, but all he could see of the stranger was a shadow with a dark stetson that lurked by one of the stalls. "But I didn't expect to come in here and have a horse bushwhack me."

"You can never know when to expect trouble," the shadow commented as it slowly approached. "So it's best to be prepared for it all the time."

Then the lamplight touched the man's face, revealing a sandy-haired head with a drooping mustache highlighting a mouth which presented a wide grin. He stood well over six feet and his chest and shoulders were impressively wide and well-developed. The green bandana around his neck matched the hat band around his black stetson. A glance at the ornate green shamrock on the walnut grips of the man's .44 pistol holstered at his hip would have confirmed his identity, but Clint had already recognized Warren Murphy.

They'd once faced each other in the streets of Avalon, New Mexico, prepared to draw and fire in a lethal contest that would have cost one of them his life if the gunfight hadn't been canceled at the last moment. After meeting a man under such circumstances, one never forgets his face for it once had *death* written all over it.

However, there was nothing threatening about the good-natured grin Warren Murphy displayed as he extended a hand to the Gunsmith. "When I saw that wagon and your big black gelding, I knew who it had to be."

"You were lucky, Murph." Clint smiled, shaking the hand of the man known as the Irish Gun. "I didn't have any warning you were on Jarrad's payroll."

"I just arrived a while back," Murphy replied. "When I got the job offer a couple days ago, I thought it over and decided to take it. Damn near got my head shot off on my way here. Some of those fellas stationed along the wire are mighty jumpy. If I hadn't had my shamrocks on my gear, they probably wouldn't have believed me when I said why I was here."

"I thought you didn't like being called the Irish Gun."

"When it keeps me from getting shot at, I don't mind at all," Murphy answered. "The cantina's open. Buy you a drink for old time's sake?"

"Yeah," Clint agreed. "And maybe we should talk about this job we've gotten ourselves into."

The two men walked to the cantina. The interior was simple with a few wooden tables and chairs, a plain bar and a weary bartender who looked like a half-starved prairie buzzard. Two other men sat at a table playing poker for matchsticks as Clint and Murphy approached the bar.

"Whiskey or beer, gents," the bartender told them. He wasn't asking them a question. He'd just given them the selection—take it or leave it.

"Whiskey," Murphy replied.

"Beer," Clint added.

The vulture-faced bartender muttered something under his breath, probably perturbed that he had to prepare two different drinks instead of just pouring both from the same bottle or beer keg. Murphy paid the bartender and joined Clint at a table near a corner. Both men moved their chairs to have their backs to the wall.

"Heard a few stories about you after we left Leadtown," Murphy commented, referring to Avalon by its infamous nickname. "Still can't keep away from trouble, can you?"

"Happens some times." The Gunsmith shrugged.

"Heard about Hickok." Murphy looked down at his drink. "I know he was a friend of yours. Sorry, Clint."

The Gunsmith nodded. "Yeah," he replied because there was nothing else to say. "What about you, Murph? You still a gun-for-hire?"

Murphy shrugged. "That's why I'm here."

"To drive off rustlers?"

"Or shoot them." The Irish Gun grinned.

"Not exactly your line of work is it?"

"I wouldn't expect it to appeal to a traveling gunsmith either," Murphy replied. "Guess a thousand dollars sounds pretty good to just about anybody these days."

"Can't deny that," Clint confessed. "How much do you know about Jarrad and his crew?"

"About as much as you do," Murphy replied. "Just enough to wind up here."

"Did you know they've hired Parako?"

Murphy sneered. "Parako's a goddamn kid looking for a reputation, but he's got everything he needs to get one from what I've heard about the guy. Parako has to be pretty good to take John Murdock. Of course—"

The door opened and a small, emaciated dark man with incredibly wrinkled skin began to enter. The bartender immediately hurled an empty shot glass at the Indian, who hastily retreated from the cantina when the glass exploded against the door frame.

"Goddamn it!" the bartender screamed. "You know I don't let your kind in here! Goddamn digger!"

"Digger?" Murphy raised his eyebrows.

"The old guy is probably a Paiute. Some of them have taken to farming like white men, but most still struggle to survive out in the desert. They run around half naked and use sharpened sticks for a combination tool and weapon. Just about live on whatever they can dig out of the ground—muddy water, sagebrush and an occasional raw lizard."

"Digger, huh?" Murphy muttered as he finished his drink. "Figure we should get our gear and move into one of the bunkhouses for now?"

"Yeah," Clint agreed. "I'd sort of appreciate having somebody around I know well enough to be able to *almost* trust."

"Aw, hell, Clint," Murphy said. "Don't tell me you've got hard feelings about what happened back in Leadtown. So we were going to kill each other—that was just business."

"I know, Murph," the Gunsmith said. "I understand why you were going to draw on me, but that doesn't mean I liked it."

"I didn't like doing it," Murphy assured him. "But it was still—"

"Business," Clint sighed. "I know."

The pair left the cantina. The sky had darkened and a display of stars and the quarter moon again dominated the night, although a scarlet haze of stringy clouds draped many of the heavenly bodies.

"Blood on the moon," Murphy noticed. "Suppose to be a bad omen."

"You superstitious, Murph?" Clint inquired. "Don't you have faith in your lucky shamrocks?"

"My shamrocks are only lucky because they're attached to guns that I can use well enough to make my own luck," Murphy replied gruffly. "Besides, I figure if a red moon is a bad omen, it has to also be a good omen for somebody else. I just hope that somebody else is us."

NINE

Clint and Warren Murphy entered one of the bunk-houses, carrying their saddlebags over their shoulders. Murphy also had his Winchester with a shamrock on its buttstock and the Gunsmith carried his Springfield .45 carbine. The bunkhouse wasn't very large, consisting of a single room with six bunks stacked doubledecker, a small table, two chairs and a potbellied stove.

Three men were already there. Two of them were stationed by the table—a skinny character with a rat face and a mouthful of buckteeth, and a plump fellow with a flattened nose that seemed to cover most of his face. The third man stood in the center of the room. He was almost six foot five and resembled a trained bear with his huge, powerful physique and shaggy black hair and beard.

"Howdy," Murphy said. "Any vacancies in here?"

"Vacancies?" the chubby man smiled as he sat at the table and picked up an old Remington revolving rifle. "I figure we got the only two empty bunks in the place."

"That's right, Herm," the rat-faced fellow agreed. "You fellers just stash yore gear and get comfortable."

"Much obliged," Clint replied.

Then he heard Herm cock back the hammer of his rifle. The muzzle of the Remington was pointed at the

Gunsmith's chest. Another gun hammer clicked as the
rodent-faced man aimed a revolver at Warren Murphy.

"If you guys are trying to be funny," Clint began, "try
pointing those things in another direction and stick to
telling jokes."

"Ain't no joke," Herm warned. "You fellers drop
yore gear—'specially them rifles—and get yore hands
over yore heads. Pronto!"

Clint and the Irish Gun obeyed. "Mind telling us what
this is about?" Murphy asked.

"You two jaspers is new here," Herm explained. "We
don't like havin' somebody we don't know packin' a gun
when we're tryin' to relax after a long hard day. Know
what I mean?"

"It ain't polite to deny the request of yore host," the
scrawny man said with an unwholesome giggle.

"Jed's tellin' you true." Herm smiled. "Fact is, you
fellers could get killed if'n you decide to be rude with us.
Now, Jed and me is gonna keep you both covered while
Bear takes yore guns and puts 'em on this here table. You
don't try nothin' and you'll get to go to sleep tonight in a
bed instead of a coffin."

Jed giggled at the remark, but his hand remained rock
steady as he aimed his Whitney Colt at Murphy's chest.
Bear, the muscle-bound mountain man, lumbered forward and stepped behind Clint and Murphy. He plucked
each man's pistol from its holster and then placed the guns
on the table beside Herm.

The fat man leaned his arm on the edge of the table, his
hand still resting on the frame of his rifle, finger on the
trigger, but he uncocked the hammer and the muzzle now
pointed lazily in the direction of Clint Adams instead of
directly at his chest. Jed giggled once more as he holstered
his Colt.

"There." Herm grinned, leaning back in his chair to

lift the first two legs from the floor. "Ain't this more friendly?"

"If we introduce ourselves," Murphy began, "will you guys figure you know us well enough to let us have our guns back?"

Bear responded by pushing Murphy forcibly across the room. The Irish Gun was a big man, but he was dwarfed by the huge, shaggy brute. Bear smiled at Murphy and held out his large, unwashed hands.

"I ain't got no weapon, sonny," the mountain man rasped in a gravelly voice. "Makes us even if'n you wanta try me."

Clint turned to Herm and Jed. "We came in here looking for a place to sleep, not trouble from the very people we're suppose to be working with—"

"Could be you're lookin' for somethin' else," Herm declared. "Like maybe a bounty or two?"

"Hell," Murphy began, his eyes locked on Bear. "We're not bounty hunters, for Christ's sake."

"And you'd admit if if'n you was?" Jed snorted.

"You lookin' for a place to sleep, sonny?" Bear growled as he approached Murphy. "Then you take that one."

The mountain man pointed a dirty thick finger at a pair of bunks. "The top one," he continued. "Bottom bunk belongs to me. You savvy?"

"Thanks," Murphy muttered. "Can I put away my gear first?"

Bear swept a big deerskin boot into the saddlebags on the floor and kicked them into a corner. Herm and Jed laughed, but neither man took his eyes off Clint Adams, who still stood in front of the table. Herm's thumb moved to the hammer of his Remington and his finger remained curled around the trigger.

"There." Bear smiled. "It's all put away. Now, get

your ass in that bunk like a good boy, sonny.''

Murphy sighed and turned to the bunks. He seized the top one and placed his foot on the lower cot to haul himself up. Bear quickly rushed forward, seized Murphy's belt from behind and yanked hard. The Irish Gun crashed to the floor, much to the amusement of Herm and Jed.

"I told you that bottom bunk belongs to me!" Bear roared. "You better watch where you put yore big feet, sonny!"

Warren Murphy's face clouded with anger as he glared up, but his expression became impassive when he rose to his feet. Bear stomped closer and folded his thickly muscled arms on his big chest. Murphy calmly dusted his sleeves and nodded at the mountain man.

"Okay, mister," he told Bear, gesturing with his arms extended, the palms held up in a helpless manner. "I don't want any trouble with you, so I'll watch where I put my big feet—"

Then he kicked Bear between the legs as hard as he could. The big man gasped in agony, his eyes swelling in their sockets, mouth forming a black oval in his hairy face as he started to fold at the middle and clutch at his groin. Murphy's right fist shot out and hit the mountain man between the eyes. Bear staggered two steps, shook his head and bellowed with rage before he charged forward like a deranged bull.

Clint Adams didn't see Warren Murphy deftly sidestep the mountain man's rush. He barely noticed the crash of the big man's bulk connecting with the potbellied stove. The Gunsmith's attention remained on Herm and Jed.

"Son of a bitch!" Herm gasped as he began to raise his rifle and cocked the hammer.

Clint moved in swiftly, catching the barrel in his left hand to yank it toward the ceiling. Herm's finger tight-ened around the trigger and the gun bellowed, blasting a .44 lead ball into the clapboard overhead.

The Gunsmith's right fist rammed into Herm's mouth. The chair tipped over backward and man and furniture hit the floor. Clint quickly twisted the Remington from the dazed gunman's grasp. Holding the rifle by its barrel, the Gunsmith raised it like a butter churn and stamped the buttstock under Herm's breastbone.

As the fat man gasped and convulsed on the floor, clawing at his solar plexus and coughing on vomit, Jed hastily yanked his Whitney Colt from its holster. He swung the pistol toward Clint and began to thumb back the hammer. The Gunsmith reacted faster. He pivoted and chopped the barrel of the Remington rifle across Jed's wrist. The Whitney Colt dropped from the gunman's hand. Jed cried out in fear and alarm. Then Clint silenced him with a rapid butt-stroke to the man's ratlike face. Walnut smashed into buckteeth and Jed was propelled into a wall where he slumped in an unconscious heap on the floor.

Clint turned to see Bear swing a wild right cross at Warren Murphy's head. The Irish Gun nimbly dodged the mountain man's ham-size fist and hooked a solid right to Bear's solar plexus, followed by a left to a kidney. Bear half gasped and half bellowed. He slashed a backfist at Murphy, who again avoided the attack and drove an uppercut under the larger man's ribcage.

Bear moaned and folded at the middle. Murphy's left arm quickly shot out and snaked around the brute's furry head to apply a head lock—just long enough to smash his right fist into Bear's face. Then Murphy pivoted, grabbed Bear's greasy hair in both hands and shoved his head down to meet a folded knee which crashed into the mountain man's bearded jaw. Bear fell like a lightning-struck redwood tree. The bunkhouse seemed to tremble from the impact of the big man hitting the floor.

"Isn't it nice to meet new people?" Clint commented dryly as he handed Murphy his shamrock-decorated .44 pistol. The Gunsmith already had his own double-action Colt in his fist.

"Great," Murphy replied sourly, taking his gun.

Clint relieved Jed and Herm of their firearms, checking them for holdout weapons, finding a derringer in the fat man's boot. Murphy made a similar search of Bear and found a bowie knife sheathed at the small of his back. They placed the weapons on the table.

"Now what?" Murphy wondered, holstering his revolver.

"Maybe we should sleep under the stars tonight," Clint suggested.

"Yeah," the Irish Gun agreed with a sigh.

Suddenly, the door burst open and a figure appeared at the threshold. The new arrival held a .45 Colt aimed at the Gunsmith and Warren Murphy, but the man's youthful features seemed to present as great a threat as the weapon in his hand. His face seemed to be chiseled out of pale stone, with thin lips, flared nostrils and hard black eyes.

"Troublemakers, huh?" the young gunman whispered as a cold smile slithered across his colorless lips. "Know how we handle troublemakers here?"

He thumbed back the hammer of his Colt.

TEN

"Parako!" a voice barked. "Put that gun away!"

The young hardcase stiffened, but he didn't holster his weapon and his onyx eyes remained locked on Clint and Murphy. "These fellers got some explaining to do."

"We can talk without having a gun pointed at us," Clint told him.

"Adams?" Baltimore Smith appeared at the doorway. "What are you doing here?"

"Right now I'm wishing this guy would put his gun away," Clint replied dryly.

"Parako!" Smith snapped.

Reluctantly, the young gunman slid his Colt into its holster. "You call this feller Adams?"

"Clint Adams," Smith confirmed. "Who are you, fella?" he asked Murphy.

The Irish Gun introduced himself.

"Glad you could make it." Smith nodded. "Now, what happened here?"

"Some antisocial behavior," Clint replied. "But we didn't kill anybody for it."

"This time," Murphy added.

"The Gunsmith and the Irish Gun," Parako remarked with a sly smile. "Well, well, looks like we really are

47

gettin' some professional help here. What's a feller supposed to say to a couple of famous living legends like you two?''

"Hello is all right," Murphy told him.

Herm began to sit up, rubbing his fat belly as he turned his head to one side and threw up. Bear stirred slightly and Jed began to moan, probing his bloodied mouth with his fingers.

"They don't seem to be hurt too bad," Smith commented, expressing little concern for their condition.

"They won't be feeling too frisky for a while." Clint shrugged. "But they only lost a few teeth, not their lives."

"You two aren't suppose to be here anyway," Smith stated. "Get your belongings and we'll head back to the house."

"Good." Clint nodded. "I think we should have another chat with Mr. Jarrad."

The Gunsmith and Warren Murphy followed Baltimore Smith and Parako to the ranch house. Alfred Jarrad met them at the door. Dressed in a purple robe, the rancher padded onto the porch in slipper-clad feet and demanded to know what had happened. Clint Adams answered him, neither exaggerating the incident nor distorting the facts. Murphy had nothing to add, so he simply listened and nodded in agreement with Clint's version.

"Thought you two were experts with guns, not with your fists," Jarrad remarked. "Taking on three men with your hands and coming out without a scratch is pretty impressive fisticuffs."

"We're pretty impressive fellas," Murphy said with a shrug. "And if you think that's something, you ought to see what we can do with our guns."

"I'm looking forward to it," the rancher replied.

"What concerns me, Mr. Jarrad," Clint began, "is the

fact those men thought we might be bounty hunters. What sort of men are you hiring and what kind of work are they supposed to do?''

''I told you before, Adams,'' Jarrad said. ''I'm protecting my property. Some of the men I've hired might have a tainted past, but as long as they behave themselves while they're here, I don't really care about that.''

''You don't care if you've got a bunch of cutthroats on your payroll?'' Clint inquired.

Jarrad smiled. ''Not as long as I can make sure they toe the line, Adams.'' He strolled inside the house. ''Besides, you two won't have to stay in the bunkhouse with the common help. Eliza has already prepared your quarters here.''

''In the house?'' Murphy raised an eyebrow.

''Naturally,'' Jarrad confirmed. ''I want my best men to receive the best of treatment. Baltimore, show them to their rooms.''

''I can do it, Mr. Jarrad,'' Parako declared eagerly.

''You're watch commander tonight,'' the rancher told him. ''Besides, I gave the order to Baltimore, not you.''

''Yes sir,'' the young gunhawk muttered sourly. Then he turned and galloped off the porch.

Clint and Murphy followed Jarrad and Smith into the house. The rancher led the way up the stairwell, which proved to be larger than the Gunsmith had realized, consisting of more than two dozen steps and two landings. At the head of the stairs, Jarrad handed a kerosene lantern to Smith.

''I can find my way to my room from here,'' he said. ''See to our guests, Baltimore.''

''Father?'' a soft feminine voice called from the shadows of the upstairs hallway.

Sylvia, dressed in a loose-fitting white robe, appeared from the darkness like an apparition. The ghostlike impression was only slightly diminished when the lamplight struck her pale, lovely face. Clint realized that until now he hadn't heard her utter a word. The girl had been strangely silent during the evening meal, so silent, in fact, Clint had wondered if she could speak.

"Is everything all right, Father?" the girl inquired.

Her voice had an elegant quality that revealed a formal education, probably by tutors from the East. She did not seem to express fearful concern as most women might after hearing an unexpected gunshot in the middle of the night. Sylvia had calmly asked a question. She might have been referring to rain clouds in the night sky.

"Yes, dear," Jarrad assured her. "A couple of our new men had a disagreement with some of the boys in the bunkhouse. No one was hurt and it's over now."

"I take it Mr. Adams was involved in the trouble," she commented, turning to face Clint.

"We weren't exactly welcomed by the current residents," the Gunsmith explained.

"But you weren't harmed and you took care of them easily enough, didn't you?" A trace of amused satisfaction seemed to flavor her words.

"I think you'd better get back to bed, dear," Jarrad advised.

The girl's ghostly form melted into the shadows and a door closed gently. Alfred Jarrad's departure was equally abrupt, although it lacked his daughter's haunting, catlike grace as he marched down the hallway and slammed a door shut.

"In case you didn't hear, Murphy," Baltimore Smith said, "that's the boss's daughter."

"Figured she was either his daughter or wife or something like that," the Irish Gun replied. "I'd keep away from her even if she wasn't kin to Jarrad."

"Oh?" Smith remarked. "Then you're the first fella I've met who isn't attracted to Sylvia."

"I didn't say she isn't attractive," Murphy explained. "I just said I'd keep away from her."

Clint Adams was only mildly surprised by Murphy's comment. He had also felt oddly uneasy around the beautiful, yet strange young woman. Something about her reminded him of the myths about the Sirens, beautiful sea nymphs who lured sailors with their magical songs, causing the men to dash their ships upon rocky reefs.

Yet, that very attribute of feline grace and probable cunning contributed to Sylvia's magnetism. Murphy's remark about avoiding Sylvia under any circumstances was probably wise, but Clint wasn't so certain he wouldn't pursue the woman if she hadn't been Jarrad's daughter. There's always an element of risk involved with a man and a woman. Clint may have acted differently if he'd met Sylvia, temptress or not, in another place and another time.

Baltimore Smith escorted Clint and Warren Murphy to their rooms at the west wing of the house. Clint entered his new quarters and struck a match to locate a coal-oil lamp on a small table in the center of the room. He managed to keep the flame from dying long enough to light the lamp. The place was pleasantly furnished with a brass bed, a chest of drawers, a washbasin with a pitcher and a small desk.

Clint stashed his saddlebags in a corner and placed his Springfield carbine on the floor by his bed. He unbuckled his gunbelt and hung it over the headboard so it would be within easy reach while he slept. Then he put out the lamp, stripped off his clothes and climbed into bed.

Within minutes, he was asleep, resting in a modified slumber, his senses still keenly alert although his nerves and muscles rested. Long ago he'd had to develop this form of survival sleep for he was not a man who could afford to drop his guard even when he rested.

Yet he didn't hear the door open or sense the intruder's presence until cool fingertips brushed his cheek. Clint awoke with a start, his hand automatically flying to the holstered Colt near his head. A woman's gentle laughter arrested his action.

"Do you really think you'll need that, Clint?" Sylvia Jarrad asked as she stood beside his bed.

ELEVEN

The Gunsmith didn't know how to reply to her question, but he moved his hand away from the butt of his pistol. Sylvia sat on the edge of the bed. The girl's platinum hair and pale complexion were as starkly visible in the darkness as her white robe, yet her dark violet eyes seemed almost hollow in the dim light.

Clint felt as if he was being visited by a seductive female demon. It thrilled yet frightened him at the same time.

"I may call you Clint?" Sylvia whispered, slowly peeling the sheet back.

Clint was even more confused about what to say or do. Should he ask what she wanted or warn her that he was naked underneath the sheet? Should he tell her to leave or surrender to the odd attraction he felt which combined lust with apprehension and desire with foreboding.

"Yes, you may call me Clint," he replied at last. "Sylvia?"

She laughed again and began to run her fingers across his chest, combing hair with her nails. Clint trembled, yet even he could not say if it was due to sensual pleasure or fear. Fear? The Gunsmith never would have believed he could be so unnerved by an unarmed woman, yet he'd never encountered one even remotely similar to Sylvia Jarrad.

"I make you nervous, Clint," she said, her hands sliding along his stomach. "You're not afraid of me, are you?"

"Should I be?" he replied.

"I didn't come here to hurt you, Clint," she assured him, her hands reaching between his thighs to caress his erection.

"Why . . ." Clint chuckled. "Hell, I almost asked why you're here."

"That's obvious," she said. "Isn't it?"

Then she lowered her head to his crotch. Clint gasped as she slowly tongued his stiff member. Sylvia's cool lips slipped over the head of his penis. *Jesus*, he thought. *This must be a dream. This can't be happening.* Yet, the fiery desire in his loins was real enough and so was the lovely woman who serviced him.

Her teeth gently chewed him, gradually increasing pressure. Clint stiffened when her nips began to pinch skin. My God! How badly could she hurt him with those teeth? Ordinarily, he wouldn't even consider such a ghastly action by a woman, but Sylvia was so strange, so unlike any woman he'd known before.

His fears proved groundless, however, as she stopped using her teeth and carefully caressed his maleness with her tongue and lips, drawing him deeper into the warm cavern of her mouth. The tension oozed from Clint Adams and only erotic pleasure remained as she kissed and sucked, his member swelling until it threatened to burst.

"Sylvia," he whispered hoarsely.

She withdrew her lips from his penis and smiled at him. The girl untied the cord of her robe and rose to shed the garment. The Gunsmith stared at her beautiful naked body and wondered once more if it could be a dream.

Her pale skin seemed unnaturally smooth and flawless. Sylvia's breasts were large, but firm, with proud pink nipples mounted high on their globular mounds. The girl's figure was perfect, with a trim waist and hips that matched the swell of her breasts. Long curved legs extended to alabaster thighs with a patch of white-gold hair between them.

Sylvia slid into the bed beside Clint and snaked her arms around his neck as he embraced her. Their lips crushed together and he felt Sylvia's tongue work within his mouth while her fingernails coasted along the curve of Clint's spine at the small of his back. Sylvia slid a leg across his thigh, pulling him closer to grind herself against his stiffened manhood.

Clint wasn't usually the passive partner when making love, and as soon as he recovered from the initial surprise of the bizarre encounter, he assumed the dominant role.

He began to kiss her long ivory neck while his hands found her breasts, fondling gently and teasing the nipples until they were stiff and hard under his fingers. Slowly, his lips moved along her throat. The girl moaned with pleasure and Clint continued to slide his hands lower while his mouth descended to her breasts. He kissed and nibbled her milk-white flesh as his hands found her thighs and stroked the smooth warm skin before inserting two fingers into the center of her womanhood.

Sylvia groaned and began raking her nails across Clint's back. His hand moved faster, drawing his fingers to and fro within her. Clint slowly removed his hand and straddled Sylvia's upper torso, placing his erection between her breasts. Taking her firm mounds in his hands, he gently pressed them together, moving his stiff penis back and forth within the tunnel of flesh.

"Oh, Clint," she moaned, trying to seize his member, her hungry mouth open to receive it once more.

However, the Gunsmith rose and quickly altered his position on the bed, turning himself around to lower his face into Sylvia's crotch while placing his legs on either side of her head. The girl's mouth again found his penis and drew on him with passionate skill.

Clint's mouth moved to her love triangle. He kissed the pale hairy patch and probed along the lips of her vagina with his tongue. The scent of her musky womanhood filled his nostrils as he inserted his tongue and lapped at her hot damp portal. Sylvia gently gnawed his maleness as the thrusts of his tongue became faster and drove deeper within her.

He felt her body buck and tremble and realized she was approaching an orgasm. Sylvia's lips slid up and down the length of his shaft and he too neared the brink of endurance. Yet, he hastily arched his buttocks to pull himself from her mouth, again fearful of her teeth, aware she might unintentionally bite down in the heat of passion.

Then he heard her cry out in ecstasy. Clint turned around once more and now entered her. Clint fought to control his fiery desire as he rotated his pelvis to work his erection slowly into her love chamber.

But the girl didn't want it slow. She instantly began bucking and convulsing beneath him, drawing him deeper inside. Sylvia groaned and dug her nails into his shoulders and biceps. Her legs snaked around his hips, pulling him deeper. Clint held back as long as he could before his seed exploded within the girl. Riding his still hard, throbbing member, she reached a second orgasm and twisted violently as a spasm of pleasure swept through her strong, firm body.

"That was wonderful, Clint," Sylvia crooned. "Thank you."

"The feeling's mutual," he assured her.

"Good," she grinned. "And you don't seem to be nervous anymore."

"Frankly," Clint began. "there's something that still has me confused. Why did you—"

"Throw myself at you?" Sylvia supplied.

"I wouldn't put it that way exactly."

"Oh? How would you put it?"

"I'd try not to."

"The question is the same regardless of verbal window dressing," Sylvia declared. "So is the answer. I wanted you. Isn't that enough?"

"I don't have anything to complain about," he chuckled. "Except for the fact you scared the hell out of me when I woke up and found you in my room."

"That was careless of me," she replied. "I apologize."

"And I'm embarrassed," Clint admitted. "I'm a pretty light sleeper. I wouldn't have thought an Apache could have sneaked up on me the way you did."

"I'm very good at being quiet," Sylvia told him. "I had to learn how to be quiet a long time ago."

"Really?" Clint asked, intrigued by the lovely, passionate, yet mysterious woman.

"Yes," she whispered. "But now I'd better return to my room. Sleep well, Clint Adams, and thank you."

"No need to—" he began as she slithered off the bed with uncanny speed and grace. He seemed to blink and suddenly she was once again dressed in her robe and standing by the bed.

"And take care, my lover," she said sharply.

With that, she hurried on silent cat feet to the door and departed. Clint thought about the encounter and her parting words. The warning seemed anything but casual. Another cold shiver rode along the Gunsmith's spine and he knew he'd get very little sleep that night.

TWELVE

The following morning, Clint and Warren Murphy were taken on a complete tour of the Big J with Baltimore Smith for a guide. Again, Clint noticed the easterner's surprising prowess as a horseman as they galloped along the fence, checking guard stations located throughout the perimeters of Alfred Jarrad's spread.

"We have men posted every mile," Smith explained. "Three man teams at each station. They're close enough to each other so another team can come to a distressed group if they hear any shooting."

"Isn't that sort of excessive?" Warren Murphy remarked as he leaned against the horn of his saddle. The Irish Gun still rode the same handsome roan gelding he'd had when Clint first met him in Leadtown.

"This property and those cows"—Smith pointed at a herd of Longhorns with about a hundred fat white-faced Herefords scattered among them—"are worth a lot, Murphy."

"Yeah." Murphy nodded. "But all this security in broad daylight—"

"Who says rustlers only strike after dark?" Smith inquired. "If nothing else, we have to keep an eye out for the Paiutes. Those goddamn diggers are so frightened of evil spirits and goblins and whatever else they believe in, they'd never dare try anything at night. But they're still sneaky bastards and they might just try something in the daylight.''

"I don't think a bunch of scrawny Indians armed with sharpened sticks are going to try to steal any of these cows,'' Clint said as he patted Duke's neck.

"A lot of Paiutes have turned farmer recently,'' Smith declared. "Some of them, mostly half-breeds, know how to use guns.''

"And I'd guess they'd be even less likely to be cattle rustlers.'' Clint shrugged. "Anyway, what are Murph and I supposed to do to earn our keep around here?''

"You'll be watch commanders like Parako,'' Baltimore Smith answered. "You'll check on the guard posts to make sure the men are alert. Check for breaks in the wire and always''—he turned to stare at both men— "*always* expect trouble.''

"How many incidents of rustling have occurred here?'' Murphy asked.

"Enough to make it clear that all these precautions are necessary,'' Smith replied.

"How many men have been killed by the rustlers?'' Clint inquired.

"I don't really know,'' Smith admitted. "But you'd better believe this is a serious job with real dangers involved.''

"Didn't figure I'd get paid a thousand dollars a month if it wasn't,'' Murphy sighed.

Smith extracted his pocket watch from his vest. "It's getting close to lunch time. Let's head back to the house.''

As Baltimore Smith galloped forward to lead the way back to the ranch Murphy steered his mount close to Clint. "We're going to get paid a hell of a lot of money and all we have to worry about are lazy sentries, a few cattle thieves and getting to the chow line on time.''

"And you figure there's more to all this than what we've been told?'' Clint asked.

"Don't you?''

"Yeah,'' Clint confessed. "The question is: What else do they want that they haven't told us and when will they break the news to us?''

"That's two questions,'' Murphy stated, his eyes wandering over Clint's magnificent black gelding. "You know, I'd pay you five hundred dollars for that horse.''

"*That's* not even a question,'' the Gunsmith stated. "But I can answer you anyway—Duke isn't for sale for any price.''

"If you get killed, can I have him?''

"That would be up to Duke,'' Clint replied with a straight face.

THIRTEEN

Clint and Murphy caught up with Baltimore Smith and the three men rode together toward the ranch house, moving at an easy gallop as they allowed their horses to set the pace. When they saw a group of people had congregated between the cantina and the livery stable, the three men pulled back the reins of their mounts to bring the animals to a halt.

Most of the crowd looked like cowboys and hands. The congregation's attention was clearly centered on three figures who stood well apart from the others—one positioned roughly ten feet from the other two.

"What's going on?" Clint asked Smith.

"I don't know." Smith urged his horse forward at a fast gallop.

Clint and Murphy followed his example. As they drew closer, the trio recognized Parako, who stood facing two other men dressed in shabby, dirt-stained denim overalls and caps. Naturally, Parako wore his gunbelt and—judging by his stance and the way his hand hovered over his Colt—he was about to use his gun. The two men who faced him were also armed, but their hands trembled as they moved toward the butts of their holstered weapons.

Parako didn't hesitate. He drew his pistol with the

incredible speed and certainty of a professional. His gun roared and one of his reluctant opponents was thrown to the ground by a .45 caliber bullet in the chest. The other man was still desperately clawing at his yet-holstered revolver when Parako fired again. The second man was hurtled backward, his hands clawing at a crimson geyser that sprouted from a bullet hole in the center of his throat. Then the man collapsed beside his slain companion.

"Yah-hoo!" Parako exclaimed. "You see that? I gunned 'em both down afore they could even clear leather! Told you I could do it, didn't I?"

"Yes, you did," a woman's voice replied weakly.

"Did you take the picture?" Parako demanded. "I was kinda busy so I couldn't be sure if'n you did or not."

"Uh . . . no," the woman said. "It all happened too fast. I'll . . . take the photograph now."

"Let me get over next to 'em," the young gunman urged as he walked to the two men he'd killed.

While Parako propped up the corpses into a seated position, the crowd began to dissolve. A woman clad in a blue dress was stationed behind a camera mounted on a tall tripod. Her head and shoulders were buried under a black cloth. She held a T-shaped flash rod in one hand as she focused the lens under the ebony sheet.

"It can't be her," Clint whispered to himself, but he knew his comment was wishful thinking.

Parako stood behind his victims, proudly holding his Colt revolver against his chest. The dead men leaned against the killer's legs. Blood stained their shirts and their eyes were wide open in the astonished manner of the newly dead. *Trophies*, Clint thought. That's all killing those two men meant to Parako—a chance to claim a couple more trophies and to carve two extra notches on the grips of his six-gun.

Then the phosphorus powder popped into a brilliant

burst of white at the top of the flash rod as the girl took a
photograph of the brutal young man who killed in order to
build a reputation for murder. Clint held his breath as the
girl slipped the cloth from her head. He hoped against
hope that he'd guessed wrong about her identity.

He hadn't.

Darlene Farrell had arrived at the Big J.

FOURTEEN

"What the hell is going on here?" Baltimore Smith demanded as he stopped his quarter horse near Parako.

"Shouldn't oughta talk that sort of language around a lady, Baltimore," the young gunhawk declared as he dramatically thrust his Colt into its holster. "Might not be healthy."

"Shit!" Smith snarled, swinging down from his mount. "If she doesn't mind taking pictures of killings for a living, she can damn well put up with a little rough language."

Parako kicked one of the corpses aside as he marched toward Clint and Warren Murphy. "You two see what I done? Took on two fellers in a fair gunfight and beat 'em fair and square!" he said proudly.

"Yeah," Murphy replied dryly. "And both of them looked like they know enough about guns to reach for the right end to grab onto."

"Why'd you kill them, Parako?" Clint demanded as he swung down from Duke's back.

"It was a fair fight," Parako insisted. "I met 'em face to face and I'd given each of 'em one cartridge apiece so they could defend themselves. . ."

"Look, you nasty little bastard," Clint snapped. "You killed two men who probably knew as much about gun-

65

fighting as I know about needlepoint. Now, answer my
question—why?''

''They were cattle rustlers, Clint,'' Darlene replied.
''Mr. Parako said they'd be hanged anyway so he offered
them a chance to save themselves by facing him in a
gunfight—''

''Some chance,'' Murphy muttered sourly as he
climbed down from his roan gelding.

''And you just couldn't resist a chance to take a photograph of a real, honest-to-God Western-style killing,
could you?'' Clint glared at Darlene. ''Make a great
addition to your story for the newspaper, won't it?''

''Wait a minute!'' Baltimore Smith rasped. ''You two
know each other?''

''Mr. Adams and I met on the trail the other day,'' the
girl replied stiffly. ''Isn't that true, *Mr*. Adams?'' Darlene's eyes seemed to lance shards of anger at Clint as she
added, ''Or should I call you *the Gunsmith*?''

''Who the hell is this woman?'' Smith wanted to know.
''A goddamn newspaper snoop?''

''That's a rather accurate description,'' Clint commented, noting with satisfaction that Darlene visibly stiffened from the remark.

''How did she get in here?'' Smith demanded, glaring
at Parako.

''The lady rode down here from Silvertown,'' Parako
said. ''She'd heard tell 'bout all the famous gunmen we
got here like the Gunsmith and the Irish Gun''—his chest
swelled with pride—''and me. She figured there was a
story here so—''

''So you let her in and killed two men to entertain her.''
Clint shook his head with disgust.

''They was rustlers, damn it!'' Parako snarled, his hand
dropping to the gun on his hip. ''I've heard 'bout all the
bad talk I plan on takin' from you, Adams. You accuse me

of bein' a liar and there'll be another dead body lyin' on the ground!''

''If that happens''—Murphy chuckled—''I'll put some flowers on your grave, son.''

Parako glared at the Irish Gun and prepared to make another angry comment.

''Calm down, Parako,'' Smith urged. ''Where'd you find those two rustlers? Over by the north range?''

The young gunslinger nodded. ''We caught 'em just a couple hours ago. They'd slipped under the wire and—''

''What's special about the north range?'' Clint asked.

''It's close to the mountains,'' Baltimore Smith explained. ''The rustlers seem to favor it because it gives them plenty of cover to sneak up on the ranch.''

''Must be a lot of devotees of Hannibal among cattle thieves these days,'' Murphy commented.

''Hannibal?'' Smith frowned.

''He was a general who was around about two hundred years before the birth of Christ,'' Clint answered, surprised by Murphy's knowledge of ancient history. ''He tried to use elephants for weapons of warfare and once marched a bunch of them across the Alps.''

''Seems I had a teacher back in Baltimore mentioned the fella.'' Smith shrugged. ''What's Hannibal got to do with our rustlers?''

''Trying to sneak a couple hundred head of steers off this property and over the Silver Peak Mountains sounds like a similar feat to me,'' Murphy explained.

''I suppose the rustlers figure they'll drive the cattle off the ranch after they cut the wire and herd them across the flatlands,'' Smith stated with annoyance.

''How the hell should we know what them cow thieves is up to?'' Parako complained.

''Maybe we could have asked them,'' the Gunsmith replied. ''If you hadn't decided to show off for Darlene.''

"We asked them." Parako shrugged. "They just wouldn't answer us is all."

"Did you ask them why they were dressed like this?" Murphy inquired, gazing down at the dead men. "I never heard of rustlers wearing denim overalls and caps before."

"Maybe it was a disguise," Smith suggested. He turned to face the young gunhawk. "Parako, old man Jarrad is gonna be madder than a dog with a double dose of rabies when he finds out what you've done."

"Hold on, Baltimore—" Parako began.

"Get this female Ned Buntline outta here," the eastern gunman instructed. "Then you haul your ass back to the ranch house. Jarrad's already heard the shooting for sure and he'll want to know what happened . . . and I sure don't envy you when you try to explain this to *him*!"

"I'll escort the girl off the ranch," Clint offered. "The lady and I have to have a little chat anyway."

"I don't care if a swarm of horseflies pick her up and wing her outta here," Smith answered. "Just so long as she's gone."

"Let's go, Darlene," the Gunsmith told her.

"Aw, Clint!" she moaned, but the girl realized it was pointless to argue.

FIFTEEN

Fifteen minutes later, Clint Adams, riding on Duke alongside Darlene's horse and buggy, escorted the girl from the ranch. As soon as they were away from the place, she turned to Clint, her lovely face filled with anger.

"Now, why didn't you tell me who you really are, damn it?" Darlene demanded.

"I did." He shrugged. "I'm really Clint Adams."

"Also known as the Gunsmith."

"I don't call myself that," he replied. "Other folks gave me that handle, but that doesn't mean I have to use it."

"All right," she declared, suddenly pulling back the reins of her one-horse team to bring the rig to a halt.

"Keep moving, Darlene," Clint told her. "This is still too close to Jarrad's property and I don't think he takes kindly to trespassers."

"I noticed," she said grimly.

"Sure," Clint scoffed. "It bothered you so much you took a picture of Parako standing over the two men he'd killed. Of course, you only did that so you can show everybody who reads your paper how awful it was."

"It *was* awful," she whispered. "But I was just doing my job. Besides, Parako said they were going to hang those men if they hadn't agreed to face him. . . ."

"Don't call that an execution." Clint jerked his head toward the ranch. "Parako was enjoying a little blood sport with human victims."

"If you object so strongly, why are *you* working for Jarrad?"

"After what happened today, I'm not working for him any longer."

"You intend to quit?" Darlene asked, staring up at Clint.

He nodded. "If a man doesn't live by his principles, he's not much of a man."

"What if Jarrad won't let you go?" Darlene's eyes widened in horror.

"I doubt that he'll try to stop me," the Gunsmith said. "Anyway, I'll find out just as soon as I head back and tell him I'm through. Now, you get out of here. You ought to have enough tales for your newspaper story that will please everybody back East who love to read about violence and bloodshed in the West—as if the same damn thing doesn't happen in their so-called civilized cities."

"I'll tell my story just as I've seen it, Clint," she assured him.

"Fine," he nodded. "But don't come back here looking for any additions to your article. You've managed to get out of the Big J ranch in one piece. Don't stretch your luck by going back again."

"But I don't have an end to my story—"

"Yes, you do," Clint corrected. "I'm throwing you off Alfred Jarrad's property—end of story."

"Shit!" Darlene muttered, but she whipped the reins across the mare's back to urge it into a fast gallop. The Gunsmith watched her ride out of sight before he turned Duke around and headed back to the Big J ranch.

SIXTEEN

"I quit," Clint Adams told Alfred Jarrad.

He'd located the rancher in a spacious study where Jarrad sat behind an immense walnut desk, surrounded by shelves filled with books and pewter knickknacks. One wall did little but supply a frame for a large pair of French windows. Another contained a fireplace with a family portrait hung over the mantel.

"Have a seat, Adams," Jarrad said in a low, flat voice.

"My mind's made up, sir," the Gunsmith declared. "I'm leaving."

"I'd appreciate you sitting down and hearing me out," the rancher told him. "I've shown you the hospitality of my home and I trust you'll return this courtesy by obliging me."

"Of course," Clint agreed, lowering himself into a chair in front of Jarrad's desk.

"What Parako did today was unfortunate," Jarrad began as he removed a curve-stemmed pipe from a desk drawer and opened a humidor.

"It was more than unfortunate," Clint said. "He's a professional and the other two weren't. I'd call that murder, Mr. Jarrad."

"A court would be apt to disagree with you, Adams," the rancher said, filling the bowl of his pipe.

71

"Maybe," the Gunsmith shrugged. "But I'm more concerned with my personal opinion of the matter."

"Killing is nothing new to a man like you," Jarrad remarked, striking a match to light his pipe. "And I didn't think you had a soft spot for cattle rustlers."

"Those men weren't cattle rustlers and you know it," Clint said grimly.

"Oh?" Jarrad slowly drew on his pipe. "And what do you think they were?"

"Judging from the way they were dressed, I'd say they were a couple of miners," Clint answered. "Probably digging for silver in the mountains beyond the fence."

"You're right," Jarrad admitted as a shroud of gray smoke surrounded his head. "But they were looking for their silver on *my* mountain."

"I didn't know you owned one," the Gunsmith said dryly.

"Maybe I should tell you about my mountain." Jarrad removed the pipe from his mouth and used the stem to point at the portrait above the fireplace. "First, allow me to introduce my family—as it was eight years ago."

The painting depicted a man, woman and two children. A younger version of Alfred Jarrad stared down from the portrait, his hair only sparsely streaked with gray at the temples, his jawline lean and his eyes unaided by the glasses he now wore.

Beside Jarrad stood a lovely young woman with blond hair and dark blue eyes. The resemblance to Sylvia was stunning, yet Clint realized the woman in the picture was Jarrad's wife. The two children in the painting, a boy and a girl, favored their mother. The towheaded youngsters had round, cupidlike faces with large eyes and mischievous mouths. All four were dressed in their Sunday best— a perfect model of an affluent, happy family.

"My wife, Sabrina, son Jason and, of course, Sylvia,"

Jarrad explained. "When that painting was made, we were very happy. Life was good and we had everything—money, property and each other.

"But all that changed in the months that followed," Jarrad continued. "A drought claimed most of the Great Basin and we couldn't get the grass to grow anymore. Our cattle were dying. We seemed destined to lose all that we held dear—except each other."

Clint listened attentively, noting the change in the rancher's personality. The man seated at the desk spoke softly, carefully, and his words revealed greater education and thoughtfulness than the Alfred Jarrad Clint had met the night before.

"My foreman in those days was a man named Sam Shipe, a former prospector who'd failed to find gold in California and then repeated his performance by being just as unsuccessful when he'd prospected for silver here in Nevada. Sam was sure there was precious metal to be found, however, and he believed it lay in those mountains. . . ."

Jarrad suddenly rose from behind his desk and lurched forward with a violent speed that surprised the Gunsmith. The rancher thrust his pipe at the French windows, pointing the stem at the purple mounds that lurked at the horizon beyond the green grazing land of the Big J spread.

"Those mountains," he declared savagely. "Well, we were desperate. Sam was probably wrong about the silver, we knew that, but what did we have to lose? So we made an expedition to the mountain he felt offered the greatest promise of hidden wealth. We called it the Hill of Hope. . . ."

Jarrad laughed bitterly. "The Hill of Hope," he repeated, shaking his head. "Sam and a few cowboys who'd remained despite the drought and I did the actual digging and blasting. Sabrina prepared the meals and was always on hand to tend to the numerous minor injuries caused by our amateur efforts at mining. Jason and Sylvia also tended to various chores, mostly washing dishes, inspecting rock samples for traces of silver ore and carrying water to the men. We were quite industrious, working like pack mules in the blistering heat. Sweaty, dirty men who collapsed in their cots at sundown, too fatigued to dream. . . .

"Perhaps we didn't want to dream," he reflected. "Maybe some inner warning system protected us, for a realistic dream promised only despair that our efforts would be in vain while an optimistic one would only raise hopes that would almost certainly be dashed."

Jarrad's face hardened and his eyes stared out the window at the mountains. "Some say dreams can tell us of future events. Clairvoyance it's called. If we'd received some sort of mystical message, perhaps we could have recognized it and left those mountains in time. But as I said before, we did not dream. . . ."

"What happened?" Clint asked gently.

"A Shoshoni war party attacked one night when we lay in our cots, sleeping like the exhausted beasts of burden we'd become. I awoke to see three savages burst into our tent. One of them fell upon Sabrina while the others attacked me. Before I could reach my gun, something struck my head and I lost consciousness."

Jarrad slowly raised the heel of a palm to his right temple as though the pain of that blow long ago had returned.

"I didn't awake until three days later," he continued. "A cavalry patrol had found our camp by the Hill of Hope. Sam Shipe and the other men had been slaughtered. My wife had been raped repeatedly and murdered. Jason, my son, had been slashed to ribbons by the Shoshoni and Sylvia was missing. The cavalry told me the Indians had probably taken her and they'd try to find my daughter, although they couldn't honestly offer much hope of success.''

"But they found her?" Clint asked.

"No," Jarrad replied. "A month later, we found Sylvia out there at the north range. When the Indians hit our camp that night, Sylvia had fled to the mountain—to the Hill of Hope. The Shoshoni chased her inside the mine. She ran deep into the dark tunnel we'd cut into the mountain. There was also a network of natural caves within the Hill of Hope. We hadn't dug through them because they were too small and narrow, but little ten-year-old Sylvia managed to climb into one of those cramped holes and crawled deeper into cold, damp darkness.

"She hid in the black, suffocating caverns, listening to the angry voices of the Shoshoni butchers echo within the mine. She stayed in those catacombs with nothing to eat or drink and little air to breathe. Have you ever been in a mine, Adams? The darkness is inky black. It seems as solid and thick as the rock walls that surround it. The air is stale and tastes like mildew and dust. The caves Sylvia crawled into were even worse, yet she hid within the mountain for more than a full day. Even she does not know how long she waited in that black, stony coffin until she finally ventured back to the mouth of the mine.

"It was night when she emerged and found the tattered remains of the tents, the canvas stained with blood. The Indians had left and the Army had already rescued me and taken the dead. Sylvia was alone, a frightened little girl in the dark.

"She found some food and a couple canteens the Shoshoni had overlooked. Yet, before she could eat and drink, she heard horses approach. Fearful it might be the Indians returning, Sylvia again retreated into the mine and the caves within the Hill of Hope.''

"She had to learn to be quiet," Clint whispered recalling what Sylvia had told him the night before.

If Jarrad heard him, he didn't acknowledge the Gunsmith's remark. "Sylvia didn't know what to do. Who could blame her for being disoriented and confused? The caves seemed to be a place of safety, so she remained in them for days. She found some matches among the supplies and made torches to dispel the darkness enough to explore the caves. She actually thought she might have to spend the rest of her life within the Hill of Hope.

"She finally ran out of food and water. Sylvia believed she'd die, but she didn't want to perish inside the mine. She had nowhere else to go except try to find her way back to the ranch. When we found her, she was half dead from exhaustion and malnutrition."

"She's a remarkable girl," Clint said. "You're lucky she was strong enough to survive and return to you."

"Lucky," Jarrad said bitterly. "My daughter has been marked for life by that experience. She still favors dark and silent places. To her, they still represent safety."

"How often have you let her leave this ranch to meet new people?"

"You mean men?" Jarrad glared at Clint.

"A natural interest for a girl her age to have." The Gunsmith shrugged. "She should get to meet folks outside of the Big J in order to form new friendships and—"

"How dare you tell me how to raise my daughter!" Jarrad bellowed angrily. "She's all I've got and I'll be damned—"

"Your daughter isn't your property, Mr. Jarrad," Clint replied as he rose from his chair. "She belongs to herself. So do I. Now, if you'll excuse me, I'll be on my way."

"I haven't finished talking to you, Adams!"

"Then lower your voice," Clint told him. "I'm

obliged to listen to you only as long as you behave in a civil manner.''

"Your point is well taken, Adams," the rancher nodded. "I apologize for my outburst."

"What's all this have to do with the two men Parako killed today?'' the Gunsmith asked.

"They were digging for silver in my mountain," Jarrad answered.

"It's not part of your property," Clint remarked. "Do you have legal ownership of the mountain?"

"The Hill of Hope belongs to me," the rancher insisted. "After what I went through and the suffering it brought my family, it's mine!"

"I think I've heard enough," Clint told him. "Thanks for your hospitality and please tell Sylvia I said goodbye."

SEVENTEEN

Warren Murphy met Clint when he emerged from the ranch house. The Irish Gun's horse was hitched to the rail next to Duke. Murphy grinned at Clint.

"You have a nice chat with the boss?" he asked.

"I just told him I quit," the Gunsmith replied simply.

"That's what I figured," Murphy said. "This job just doesn't seem right."

"Are you staying?"

"Hell, no." Murphy smiled. "But I don't see any reason to tell Jarrad. He'll know I'm gone when I don't show up for dinner."

"I'm going to get my wagon," Clint stated. "Which way are you headed?"

"I was thinking of heading to Las Vegas," Murphy replied. "Since the Mormons moved out, I hear it's a wide open town now. Supposed to have a cathouse with Japanese whores somewhere in that area. Ever have an Oriental woman, Clint?"

The Gunsmith chose to ignore the question. "I'm going north to the Silver Peak Range. There's bound to be some mining communities around there with men who need work done on their guns."

"Let's just get the hell out of here and decide where we'll go later," the Irish Gun advised.

"Best idea I've heard all day," Clint agreed.

Twenty minutes later, Clint and Murphy had hitched the Gunsmith's team to his wagon and prepared to leave. Baltimore Smith noticed they had gotten the rig ready to travel and approached the pair.

"Leaving, eh?" he inquired.

"Some jobs just don't work out," Clint told him.

"Neither do some employees." Smith shrugged.

"You didn't tell us about the old man's mountain," Clint said in a hard, flat voice. "Or that he has men killed for prospecting on it."

"I didn't tell you a lot of things, Adams," Smith confessed. "Planned to give you a little information at a time to see how you felt about it."

"Oh, yeah?" Murphy raised an eyebrow. "What else didn't you mention?"

"No reason to tell you now," the eastern gunman smiled. "And a lot of reasons not to tell you. Good luck to the both of you anyway."

He strode to the house, not even glancing over his shoulder at the pair. At last, the wagon was ready to travel. Clint tied Duke to the rear of the rig and Warren Murphy prepared to mount his big roan.

"Hold on, you two!" a gruff voice demanded.

Clint and Murphy turned to see Herm, Jed and Bear. The trio had apparently recovered from the thrashing they'd received. Herm and Jed dangled hands near the butts of revolvers holstered on their hips and Bear carried a Sharps Big-Fifty rifle canted on his shoulder.

"You bastards leavin'?" Jed asked with a twisted smile that displayed his split lips and jagged remains of broken teeth.

"Come to kiss us good-bye?" Murphy asked as he stepped away from his horse and dropped a hand to the grips of his pistol.

"Runnin' out on us," Bear snorted. "Figured you was yella."

"You two ain't goin' nowheres!" Herm declared, reaching for his gun.

"But you guys are," Clint told them as his fingers moved casually toward his holstered Colt. "You're about to go to the cemetery—"

Bear swung his rifle from his shoulder, catching the forestock in his left hand as he braced the butt against his hip and tried to thumb back the hammer. Herm and Jed clawed at their pistols. To some, their movements may have seemed fast and deadly. To the Gunsmith and the Irish Gun, the trio seemed rather clumsy, but just quick enough to be dangerous.

Clint and Murphy cleared leather so fast none of the onlookers even saw a blur of motion. The pistols seemed to appear in their hands as if by some sort of gunfighter's magic. The revolvers spoke so quickly, no one could be certain if the Gunsmith or Murphy fired first or how many rounds either pumped into the three fools who'd tried to take them.

Clint himself couldn't have told them much about the gun battle, except that he shot Herm in the chest, then immediately turned his attention (and the aim of his double-action Colt) toward Bear and put a .45 slug into his upper torso. He hadn't worried about Jed, certain Murphy could handle the rat-faced gunman. In fact, the Irish Gun was fast enough with his single-action pistol to take Jed and pump another round into Bear before the big man crashed to the ground.

"What the hell?" Baltimore Smith exclaimed as he bolted from the ranch house with a gun in his hand.

"They called it," Clint explained. "And lost."

"Yeah," Smith muttered as he shoved his pistol into the shoulder holster under his vest. Clint noticed the gun was a Smith & Wesson .44 with a cut-down barrel. Good man-stopper at close range. "You two ready to go?"

"And more than willing," Murphy added, returning his gun to its leather scabbard.

Baltimore Smith nodded. "Here's some advice—and you'd better take it—don't come back," he glared at both men. "Either of you."

"Don't worry," Clint assured him as he climbed onto his wagon. "I don't intend to."

But the Gunsmith would soon discover that a man's plans can change and his problems with the Big J ranch were far from over.

EIGHTEEN

The Irish Gun rode alongside Clint Adams's wagon until they'd traveled more than two miles from the Big J. Then he pulled on the reins of his horse to bring it to a halt.

"Figure it's time to part company, Clint," he announced.

The Gunsmith stopped his rig. "I thought you were heading for Las Vegas to find out about Japanese women."

"Vegas will still be there when I'm ready," Murphy stated. "Fact is, I plan to see a fella named Sapir. We might be able to do a little work together in Remo."

"You mean Reno?" Clint smiled.

"Why is everything out here named in Spanish?" Murphy shrugged. "Anyway, it's been interesting meeting up with you again, Clint."

"Yeah," the Gunsmith agreed, reaching down to shake hands with Murphy. "We made a pretty good team."

"And I'm glad we were fighting on the same side " Murphy added. "But we're both heading for different trails in more ways than one."

Clint frowned. "You're an educated man, Murph. Hell, you've got too much brains to be hiring out as a gunman."

"Look who's talking." Murphy grinned. "A traveling

82

gunsmith who attracts trouble like a long-haired dog picks up burrs.''

''Neither of us are really young enough to live the way we do,'' Clint sighed.

''Maybe. But we also got too set in our ways to change. We're a couple of loners, Clint . . . which just makes us a little better prepared than most men.''

''Prepared for what?'' Clint asked as the Irish Gun jerked the reins of his gelding to turn the animal about.

''The one thing every man has to do alone.''

Warren Murphy urged his mount forward in a fast gallop. Clint watched him depart and nodded in agreement.

''Die,'' he said simply.

NINETEEN

Clint heard the gunshots. He hauled back on the reins of his team to stop the wagon. The Gunsmith listened, recognizing the crack of rifles, occasionally accompanied by pistol shots. The sounds were coming from an arroyo several hundred yards from Clint's position.

For once, he told himself, *keep your nose out—*

Then he saw the figures of five men among a cluster of boulders on the opposite side of the arroyo. Although dressed like cowboys, the expressions of cruel pleasure that filled their faces marked them as natural-born killers. The men rushed from their shelter to dash for the arroyo, waving their rifles like savages with spears about to perform a tribal war dance.

Clint urged his wagon forward, forgetting his previous vow not to get involved. Drawing closer, he saw the object of the cowboy-killers' eager attention. In the middle of the dry, hard bed of the arroyo, a buckboard lay on its side with two dead horses still hitched to the rig. A pair of still figures lay on the ground beside the wagon.

Another figure, however, was still on her feet. Even if the girl's long black hair hadn't extended to the small of her back and an ample bosom didn't fill her denim shirt magnificently, there could be no doubt about the lone defender's sex. Her Levi's tightly fit her long, well-formed legs and a rear end that any man would love to have in his lap.

But the five men who charged into the arroyo didn't seem impressed by the girl's endowments. They dashed to her position behind the cover of the buckboard, circling the lopsided vehicle to close in from both sides. The girl held a Winchester carbine which had either jammed or run out of ammunition.

Not that this kept her from putting up a fight. Moving with the speed and grace of a puma, the girl seized the barrel of her Winchester and swung it like a bat, smashing the walnut stock into the grinning face of one of her assailants. The man dropped to one knee with a groan and she chopped the edge of the rifle butt into the base of his skull.

"Red nigger bitch!" a man's voice snarled.

The four remaining adversaries approached the girl with cautious respect and surrounded her, holding their own rifles like clubs. If they'd simply charged at once and attacked in unison, they could easily have beaten her into unconsciousness or death. The men apparently wanted her alive and healthy—and the reason seemed obvious to the Gunsmith. As Clint's wagon steadily drew closer, he saw the girl's profile with its high cheekbones and strong nose—a noble, yet beautiful face.

Despite the odds, the girl didn't surrender. She managed to shatter one opponent's elbow with a butt stroke and stabbed the barrel of her Winchester into another man's belly before one of the aggressors batted the carbine out of her grasp. The fourth man dropped his rifle and pounced on her, wrapping his arms around the girl in a front bear hug.

Suddenly, he screamed and the girl struggled to free herself of his embrace. He sank to the ground in a quiver-

ing heap. The brave beauty held a bowie knife in her right
hand, the seven-inch blade stained with fresh blood.

She whirled to confront another attacker, but he'd already thrown a punch at her face. The fist connected
solidly with her cheekbone and jaw, whipping her lovely
head to the side before she half spun and fell to the ground.

Only then did the three remaining men in the arroyo
notice the Gunsmith's rapidly advancing wagon. They
turned to face him. The man who'd hit the girl stood with
his legs splayed over her body and reached for a holstered
sidearm. His friend with the broken arm tried to do
likewise while the third man raised his rifle to a shoulder.

A bellow of pain exploded from the brute standing over
the girl. She'd lashed out with a booted foot and kicked the
man hard between his widely parted legs. Clint yanked
back the reins to his team and rose from the driver's seat,
his .45 Colt already in his fist. The pistol roared and a
bullet shrieked along the metal barrel of the rifleman's
weapon before drilling a gory hole through his right
eyeball. Blood spewed from the gouged-out socket as the
man dropped his rifle and screamed once before he died.

The fellow with the broken arm immediately thrust his
uninjured appendage overhead in surrender. A horrid cry
of agony startled Clint even as he watched the girl rise
from the ground to slash her knife across the face of the
man she'd kicked in the groin. Blood gushed from a cavity
in the center of his face and his upper teeth and gums
formed a hideous grimace. The girl had hacked off the
man's nose and upper lip with a single stroke of her blade.

Clint watched the fierce young woman follow her attack with a lethal lunge, ramming the point of her bowie
into the wounded man's solar plexus. The Gunsmith
caught a movement from the corner of his eye and turned
to see that the one-armed gunman had taken advantage of

the distraction to once again reach for his sidearm. Almost casually, Clint shot him in the heart.

The Gunsmith climbed down from his wagon and descended into the arroyo, holding his gun ready in case any of the five bushwhackers proved to be playing possum—which seemed unlikely. A quick inspection assured him they were all playing dead—a role they'd continue throughout eternity.

The girl glanced up at Clint as she knelt beside the man she'd cut up like a Thanksgiving Day turkey, wiping the blade of her bowie on his shirt. She slid the knife into a sheath on her belt as she rose.

"I don't know who you are or where you came from," she said, "but I'm sure glad you happened along, mister."

"I'm Clint Adams," he replied with a smile. "And I'm glad to be of assistance, ma'am."

"My name's Carolyn Gray Fox," she explained, stepping forward and offering a friendly grin and an extended hand.

He was stunned by the change in the girl. Moments before she'd fought with a fury and skill few men could equal. Her face had been a mask of rage; she was a warrior goddess in battle. Yet her expression had softened and her manner was now mild and pleasant.

Her face was incredibly lovely. The high cheekbones suggested Indian blood—probably Cherokee or Sioux—mixed with her Caucasian ancestry, blending perfectly with her somewhat squarish Anglo jaw and straight, firm mouth. Yet Carolyn's most striking feature was her eyes. Pale, almost transparent green, their penetrating gaze seemed to drill into Clint as though she could peer through his eyes and read his mind.

A purple bruise had formed on the side of her jaw and a

droplet of blood oozed from the corner of her mouth. The sight made Clint's stomach knot, although he realized Carolyn had been tough enough to take the punch in her face and retaliate with fearful vengeance. She was still a woman and it disturbed Clint to see a woman mistreated—especially one as lovely and fascinating as Carolyn Gray Fox.

"Are you all right?" he asked.

"Oh"—she stroked the back of her hand across her mouth to wipe away the blood—"yeah. A little rattled, but okay."

"That bastard hit you pretty hard—" Clint began.

"They hit Timber and Waldo a lot harder," Carolyn replied, sadness suddenly appearing on her features.

"Who?" Clint asked.

The sinister triple-click of the hammer of a single-action revolver being eared back immediately arrested the Gunsmith's attention. He turned to see a stocky bearded figure had risen to one knee beside the buckboard. Blood trickled from a gash above his right temple, but the wound didn't prevent him from aiming a .44 Remington at Clint. The man clenched his teeth in anger and pain as he prepared to squeeze the trigger.

TWENTY

"No, Timber!" Carolyn shouted. "He's a friend!"

The bearded man blinked, puzzled and probably still dazed by the blow that had caused his head wound. Carolyn hurried toward the fellow before Clint could warn her not to make any sudden moves toward a man with a gun in his hand who is disoriented and only semiconscious. However, the fellow recognized the girl and uncocked his revolver.

"Carolyn," he croaked hoarsely. "What in blue blazin' hell happened?"

"Jarrad's men attacked us," she replied as she moved to the figure of another man who lay motionless beside the buckboard.

"I remember the shootin'." Timber nodded. "Bullets hit the hosses and they stumbled and fell takin' the wagon with 'em." He glanced about and shrugged. "Reckon this is where we wound up."

"Waldo's dead," Carolyn announced after examining the body by the buckboard.

"He sure didn't die lonely," Timber remarked, looking at the five dead men who cluttered the ground. "These fellers all bushwhackers—I hope?"

"Yeah," Carolyn confirmed. "And we have Mr.

Adams here to thank for the fact we're still alive and they aren't.''

"Please call me Clint," the Gunsmith urged.

"Well, I surely want to thank you for what you done, Clint," the bearded man said as he strode forward to shake Clint's hand, pumping his arm as if working the handle of a water pump. "My name's Caleb Barton but folks call me Timber 'cause I used to be a lumberjack up north. Anyways, we're mighty obliged to you, Clint—''

Timber's mouth fell open as realization struck home. "Clint Adams? I'll be go to hell! You're the feller they call the Gunsmith, ain't you?"

"Guilty." Clint sighed.

"The Gunsmith?" Carolyn asked with surprise. "No wonder you use a gun so well!''

"Just a minute." Timber Barton frowned. "That polecat Jarrad's been hirin' a lot of gunhawks. You wouldn't be on his payroll, would you, Clint?"

"Timber," Carolyn scolded, waving a hand at the corpses that surrounded them. "Does it *look* like he's on Jarrad's side?''

"No, I purely reckon not. Sorry, Clint. I wasn't thinkin' so good.''

"Don't apologize," Clint told him. "The fact is Jarrad *did* hire me last night, but I quit this morning.''

The Gunsmith explained how Baltimore Smith had lured him into going to the Big J ranch, supposedly to shoo away rustlers. He told how he'd seen two men gunned down by Parako which convinced him to resign.

"I'm right glad you turned him down, Clint," Timber stated. "Hate to have you agin us." He glanced at the dead men once again.

"Actually," Clint grinned. "Carolyn took care of most of them herself.''

"She's quite a woman." Timber nodded. "We didn't

want her to come along 'cause of the danger involved, but she insisted. Weren't no job for a female, but she said she could take care of herself as well as any man in the camp and weren't none of us could argue with that neither.''

''If anyone did, he'd be wrong.'' Clint looked at Carolyn who seemed embarrassed by their praise. ''I've told you just about everything I know about Jarrad, but I don't know why he'd send a group of gunmen to ambush you.''

''To keep us from getting supplies and ammunition,'' Carolyn replied. ''We're from Jackass Gap, a mining town near the Silver Peak Range.''

''And it's populated by miners who are digging at the Hill of Hope, right?'' Clint guessed.

''If'n that's what Jarrad chooses to call our mountain,'' Timber replied.

''He considers it to be his property,'' Clint replied.

''It ain't,'' Barton insisted. ''Our outfit has a rightful claim to the Jackass Mine. Got us proper papers and all from the United States Government no less.''

''We know that Jarrad tried to mine that mountain several years ago,'' Carolyn added. ''But he never staked a claim on the mine or found one ounce of silver. Besides, Thomas Watson and his father Ben started the mine we're using and it's on the opposite side of the mountain from that pitiful hole in the ground Jarrad dug before the Shoshoni wiped out his camp.''

''Jarrad's foreman had been right about the Hill of Hope,'' Clint mused. ''But they'd looked for the silver in the wrong place.''

''That's just too bad for Jarrad.'' Timber snorted.

''Yeah,'' Clint muttered. ''Too bad for his wife and kid who were killed there too. That's why Jarrad thinks he has a right to that mountain due to the sacrifices it cost him and his family.''

''That doesn't give him a right to make us suffer now,''

Carolyn declared angrily. "His hired killers have murdered half a dozen of our men—including Tom Watson."

"Tom was Carolyn's fiancé," Timber explained in a quiet voice.

"I'm sorry," Clint told her. "And I'm not saying that Jarrad's actions have any sort of justification. I'm just trying to explain how he sees things."

"Well, ain't much sense in us jawin' about this out here in the middle of Nevada's backside," Timber commented. "We've got us another dead friend to bury, a couple dead hosses and a wagon what busted two wheels when it fell into this arroyo so that means we also got us a long walk home."

"Not really," the Gunsmith corrected. "If you'll climb on my wagon, I'll give you a ride back to your camp."

TWENTY-ONE

If towns had relatives, Clint may have wondered if Jackass Gap was the little brother of Silvertown. Like its larger counterpart to the north, Jackass Gap consisted of adobe buildings instead of old army tents and makeshift tarp lean-tos. However, unlike Silvertown, Jackass Gap was not intended to be a permanent community.

Whoever designed the buildings for Jackass Gap had simply taken some realistic efforts to put up better dwellings than those found in most mining towns. The founders had realized that extracting silver out of the mountain would require more than a year of hard labor, so they'd constructed their homes to last at least that long. The simple yet sturdy adobe houses were strictly to serve as quarters for the residents. There were no stores, saloons or law office in Jackass Gap.

Clint noted with surprise that the small community had several large adobe furnaces. They were designed to smelt the silver ore. Again, he admired the wisdom and cleverness of the men responsible for the planning and building of the campsite. By smelting the silver before taking it to Carson City or wherever, the miners would receive a better price for the metal without having to pay someone else to perform the same process.

Yet, Jackass Gap was not the industrious, potentially prosperous little mining community it had been built to be. When Clint approached the hamlet, he found himself staring into the muzzles of half a dozen rifles held by hollow men. Hollow seemed the best way to describe the weary, ragtag lot who defended Jackass Gap. Their cheeks were sunken as though giant fingers had squeezed their faces. Dull eyes peered out from deep sockets, surrounded by lines and bags. Even their manner seemed hollow. Although they quickly, fearfully aimed their guns at the Gunsmith, when they recognized Carolyn and Timber, they merely lowered their weapons and silently turned away.

"What's wrong with these men?" Clint inquired as he rode into the heart of the hamlet.

"Broken spirits," Timber replied. "Poor bastards have been bustin' their butts to get some silver outta them mountains. Some of those boys been at it for years and never got anywhere until we hit the mother lode a couple weeks ago. Trouble is, Jarrad hit *us* too. Imagine how they feel after all this time to finally strike a vein big enough to make 'em all rich and they're still stuck out here and probably gonna die before another week goes by. Them boys is half starved and shit-scared."

"Carolyn! Timber!" a voice called from one of the adobe dwellings.

A tall, ruggedly handsome man with gray-streaked red hair hobbled toward the wagon. He leaned heavily on a crude crutch tucked under his left arm as he limped forward. The smile on his weatherbeaten face was a pleasant sight after their encounter with the hollow men who guarded the town.

"We heard shooting in the distance," the man explained. "I was afraid Jarrad's men had—"

"His boys bushwhacked us, sure 'nough, Ben,"

Timber confirmed as he climbed down from the rig. "They killed Waldo and the hosses and reckon we got one less wagon now. Lucky for us, Clint here come along when he did."

The elder man raised his bushy gray eyebrows as the Gunsmith stepped down from his wagon. "I'm beholding to you, sir," he said. "Carolyn and Timber are the closest thing to kin I have now and I don't know if my heart could stand to break again if I lost them. There's no way I can aptly reward you for this, but let me know any way I can try."

"You might start by calling me Clint." The Gunsmith grinned. "Only Army officers and schoolmasters like to be called sir."

"I hope it'll be as easy to grant you anything else you want, Clint." The other man smiled as he extended his hand. "My name is Benjamin Franklin Watson."

"That's a fine name," Clint replied, shaking Ben's hand.

"My family has a tradition of giving homage to our Founding Fathers by naming the children after them," Ben stated. "Although my father, George Washington Watson, warned me this could be quite a burden at times. One is bound to have to tolerate some poor jokes from time to time. If another person asks me if I've flown any kites lately, I'll be sorely tempted to shoot him."

"Maybe your family started that tradition to give their children a name to live up to," Clint suggested.

"Clint has made quite a name for hisself too," Timber declared. "You're lookin' at the Gunsmith, Ben!"

The older man's eyes widened. "Clint Adams," he said with awe.

"It's not the kind of name you try to live up to." Clint sighed. "But that's what some folks call me."

"Maybe you'd better tell me exactly what happened on the trail," Ben said grimly. "Jarrad has been hiring a lot of gunmen and the fabled Gunsmith would be just the sort of man he'd want on his side—although, I must admit, I've never heard anything about you that would put you in the same loathsome class as Con Macklin, Stansfield Lloyd or Parako."

"You bet I'm not in their class." Clint smiled coldly. "As a matter of fact, I killed two of those fellas and I might just have to take care of the third before this is over."

Ben led Clint, Timber and Carolyn to his house. The inside of the adobe structure was furnished in a spartan manner. Except for an old Army field desk which was cluttered with papers and drawings, the place was neat and clean.

Timber and Carolyn explained how Clint had come to their rescue. Both had given the Gunsmith glowing praise for his courage and skill. Clint stated that they'd exaggerated and made it clear that Carolyn deserved most of the credit.

"The lady is one hell of a fighter." He looked at the green-eyed beauty with respect and admiration. "I've never seen a woman handle a knife like she can."

"Carolyn's father was a full-blooded Cherokee," Ben explained. "He'd been in the First Cherokee Rifle Regiment during the War Between the States. I guess you know the federal government was pretty hard on the Cherokees for supporting the Confederates during the war. Carolyn's father had seen enough of his people abused by Union troops to feel a need to teach his daughter how to defend herself."

"Clint's being modest, Ben," Carolyn said. "I would have been killed if he hadn't arrived when he did."

"One thing is clear." The elder man smiled weakly.

"He's certainly not in league with Jarrad. My apologies, Clint. I hope you'll understand why I was suspicious when I learned who you are."

"Apology accepted," the Gunsmith assured him. "And under the circumstances, I don't blame you at all . . . not that I fully understand what the circumstances are."

"You have a right to that information." Ben nodded. "About a year or so ago, my son Thomas Jefferson Watson and I discovered traces of silver ore in rock samples we removed from that mountain."

He thrust a finger at the open door, pointing at the natural tower of gray and brown rock located less than a quarter of a mile from the mining camp. The mountain wasn't exceptional in appearance, less than a thousand feet high and perhaps twice that size at the diameter of its base. Yet it seemed both majestic and ominous to the Gunsmith; probably because he knew many lives had already been lost due to the Hill of Hope.

"We put together enough men and returned to prospect," Ben continued. "I'd been an officer in the Army Corps of Engineers and architect in civilian life. Geology has always been sort of a hobby of mine, but Thomas had earned a degree in both geology and metallurgy at the Cheney University of Science in Illinois. We had all the skills necessary to succeed. Now we were ready to do it.

"We built this mining community and equipped it with everything from shovels to ore cars. For months, we dynamited the mountain and tore into it with manually wielded tools. We hauled tons of rock out of that mountain, occasionally finding more traces of silver ore— enough to keep our hopes high enough to continue.

"Then, one day a mule was towing a carload of rocks within the mine. Something sent the animal into a sort of frenzy and it managed to break free of its harness, braying and kicking at the men who tried to subdue it.'' Ben laughed lightly. ''Damned if that troublesome, ill-tempered jackass didn't actually kick a chunk of rock from the side of the tunnel and expose part of the biggest silver vein since the great Comstock Lode in Virginia City.''

Clint smiled. ''I wondered why you folks named this place Jackass Gap.''

''The mule deserved something for his discovery.'' Ben shrugged. ''Unfortunately, Sean McKenna shot the poor beast.''

''Mules ain't got much use for silver no way,'' Timber Barton remarked philosophically.

''So we had discovered a fortune in silver,'' Ben continued. ''We tunneled deeper into the rocks and extracted more and more of the precious metal. We staked our claim with the government to make everything official. Then, two weeks ago, Thomas and two other men left in a wagon to take some samples of our silver ore to Carson City for evaluation. They never returned.

''Then three of our men were returning from Papa's Town with supplies. They were ambushed by some of Alfred Jarrad's killers. The men were beaten to a pulp but allowed to live so they could relay a message. Jarrad wanted us to abandon our mine and the town of Jackass Gap or he'd kill every man, woman and child in the community.

''When we didn't obey this order, Jarrad sent snipers after us. They fired at us when we were working in the mine—'' Ben patted his crippled leg— ''an incident I have good reason to recall. After Jarrad succeeded in driving us out of the mine he sent more snipers to fire down at the camp itself. That's basically been his tactics—hit and run strikes on our town and cutting us off from our supply sources, trying to drive us out by a combination of starvation and fear.''

Ben Watson sighed. "And that pretty much brings you up to date, Clint. We"re just trying to make it from one day to the next. We've rationed what food and water we have left, but it won't last much longer. None of us are really fighting men and trying to defend the camp is getting steadily more difficult. You can see what the pressure and fear have done to the men. We're low on ammunition, stamina and hope. Ironic, isn't it? We've got a ton of silver, but soon we'll be willing to trade it for a cup of water."

"Ben," Timber said stiffly, "this might be a bad time to mention this, but I reckon there ain't no good time. Clint told us he seen a feller gun down two miners at the Big J ranch."

"Kern and Bailey." The older man shook his head. "They'd left the camp yesterday after dark to go up to the mountain and scout the area to find out where Jarrad's men were stationed."

"They found them," Clint said grimly. "Or vice versa."

"So we've lost three more men," Ben said sadly.

"But Jarrad's forces have finally suffered as well," Carolyn declared. "Don't forget, they lost five men today."

"Eight," Clint corrected. "Warren Murphy and I had a brief encounter with three fellas who tried to draw on us before we left this morning. They lost."

"Murphy? The Irish Gun?" Timber whistled softly. "Gawd, I hear he's suppose to be a top-notch gunman. A real destroyer."

"He is," Clint confirmed. "But he quit when I did. Unless I've misjudged the caliber of men on Jarrad's payroll, he's only got two real professionals—Parako and a man named Baltimore Smith. Don't let his eastern background fool you. I suspect Smith is smarter and more dangerous than Parako. Parako's probably faster with a gun, but he's too short-tempered and trigger-happy to be competent. The rest are just bottom-of-the-barrel guns-for-hire.''

"But what have we got on our side?" Ben muttered.

The Gunsmith thought for a moment before he said, "Me."

TWENTY-TWO

Ben Watson and Timber Barton stared at Clint in astonishment, but Carolyn Gray Fox merely smiled and nodded. The Gunsmith's statement hadn't surprised her. She'd either guessed he'd offer to help or known in that mysterious way that women often know what a man will do.

"Are you sure you want to get involved in this, Clint?" Ben asked.

"I don't know if I'd say I *want* to exactly"—Clint shrugged—"but I've made up my mind to stay and help you folks fight Jarrad."

"Well"—Ben smiled—"we'd appreciate it more than I can tell you—and we can pay you as well. In fact, we'll give you three times what Jarrad offered—in silver."

"That sounds more than fair," Clint replied. "Now, since you're low on supplies, we'll start by adding mine to what you've already got."

"That'll help us hold out for a while," Timber agreed. "But what we need is to be able to strike back at Jarrad when his men—"

The furious neigh of an angry horse and the alarmed shouts of startled men abruptly interrupted his sentence. Clint's keen ear told him the horse's "voice" belonged to

Duke. He bolted from the house and discovered Duke was standing before three terrified miners, his powerful body raised on its hind legs while his forehooves slashed at the men like flint-capped clubs. The miners retreated from the horse. Duke braced himself on all fours and glared at them like a well-trained guard dog protecting its territory.

"Duke!" Clint called to his horse. "Take it easy, big fella."

The gelding's attitude immediately changed when he heard the Gunsmith's voice. Duke snorted at the trio of miners and stepped back to the rear of Clint's wagon as if waiting to be tied to the rig once again.

"That horse of yours is crazy!" one of the three men shouted. He was a big fellow, almost as tall as Clint with broad shoulders and a well-muscled chest, and he spoke with a thick Dublin accent.

"Like hell," Clint growled as he approached the Irishman. The other two remained behind the big man, a sure sign he was the ringleader of the little group. "What did you three do to get Duke riled like that?"

"Hold up!" Timber Barton exclaimed as he emerged from Ben's shack. "What's goin' on here?"

"This feller's crazy horse broke its reins free of that wagon and come at us like a bleedin' demon outta hell," the Irish spokesman explained.

"Take it easy, McKenna," Timber told him gruffly.

"McKenna?" Clint smiled coldly. "The same hero who shot the mule?"

"That's right!" the Irishman replied, apparently proud of the deed. "And I'm tempted to shoot that black bastard of yours as well!"

The Gunsmith glared at McKenna. "You try it and I'll kill you," he warned, his voice as cold as December death.

"Hold on!" Timber ordered, stomping between the two men. "We got us enough trouble already—"

"Duke wouldn't have behaved violently unless he had a reason," Clint insisted. "My guess is these three tried to get into my wagon to help themselves to my supplies."

"You callin' me a thief?" McKenna demanded. By now, quite a crowd had been attracted to the scene. "If'n I was wearin' a gun, I'd—"

"You'd get yourself killed, McKenna," Timber said sharply. "Unless you reckon you're good enough to take on the Gunsmith."

McKenna gulped so loudly it sounded as if he'd swallowed his Adam's apple. "Jesus," he whispered, no longer interested in showing off for the onlookers.

"All right," Clint declared, deciding to take advantage of the fact the incident had drawn attention of virtually everyone in the town. "I'm going to be in Jackass Gap until we've taken care of this trouble with Jarrad, so I want a few things understood. Nobody steals from my wagon or from anyone else. I'll share my food and water with you until we can get more supplies. Also, I want to inspect every man's weapons to make sure they're in peak condition. We can't afford to have any faulty guns jam in a firefight—"

"Who the hell put you in charge?" McKenna snapped. He saw Ben Watson hobble from his home. "You gonna let this Gunsmith character give us orders in your camp, Ben?"

"Until I hear him say something I disagree with," Watson replied with an affirmative nod.

"Thanks, Ben," Clint said before addressing the crowd once more. "After we've seen to your empty bellies and weapons, we'll see if we can't arrange a better guard watch system so you men can get adequate rest.

You won't be much use in a fight if you're half dead from exhaustion.

"And one more thing." The Gunsmith locked a frosty gaze on McKenna. "Big Mouth here started to brag about what he'd do if he was wearing a gun. Why *isn't* he packing an iron? Jarrad's got at least fifty men working for him and all of them carry guns and they won't hesitate to use them. I know. I've been at the Big J ranch and seen his killer colony myself. From now on, I don't want to see *anyone* walking around here unarmed as if we were having a church picnic."

He turned to study the faces of the crowd. Some were startled, others were just scared, but a few seemed to express a glimmer of new hope in their hollow-socketed eyes.

"You all have to accept the reality of this situation," Clint concluded. "Alfred Jarrad has declared war on you people and Jackass Gap is a potential battlefield."

TWENTY-THREE

Clint Adams was given an adobe shack to serve as a combination living quarters, gunsmith shop and command headquarters. He inspected the miners' guns, discovering that many were in need of repairs, adjustments or modifications and almost all of them needed to be thoroughly cleaned and oiled. Clint hated to see firearms neglected and mistreated. He couldn't stifle an occasional grunt of distaste or groan of disgust when he found a hammer caked with rust or a barrel clogged with dirt.

A few of the weapons looked more like garden tools than firearms. He discarded the rusty, filthy guns and issued new weapons to the miners from the supply of spare guns in his wagon. Although he didn't charge them for his gunsmith work, Clint didn't intend to give any of his firearms away for free. The miners of Jackass Gap could easily afford to buy a new gun so if they wanted decent weapons they could damn well pay for them.

Whenever possible, however, Clint wanted the men to use their own guns because they were familiar with the individual firearm's accuracy, effective range and the pull of the barrel when the gun was fired. The miners' weapons varied from old Springfield breechloaders (which Clint discarded because the single-shot long arms were impractical for combat against Jarrad's forces) to good quality Winchesters and cartridge-firing revolvers. Clint replaced worn firing pins and rusty springs to hammers and triggers. He filed down burrs on cylinder plates and repaired cracked buttstocks and broken pistol grips.

He checked ammunition, making certain none of the cartridges had warped casings or that the black powder charges in cap-and-ball revolvers didn't contain too much or too little explosives. He urged the men to keep percussion caps dry and to clean their weapons immediately after firing. He even checked gunbelts, holsters and rifle slings for signs of wear.

Clint changed the guard shifts, placing fewer men on duty at one time, but positioning them to cover more area than before. He warned his men to remain near cover in case of a shooting match with Jarrad's men and not to investigate strange sounds or suspicions on their own.

"Report back to us and we'll check it out with enough men to fight a possible ambush," he explained. "I'd rather we send a patrol out to find a jackrabbit chewing on some sagebrush than to have one of you wander off alone and get his throat slit."

They practiced drills so each man would know his position in case of an attack, thus preventing the enemy from using a two-prong assault, drawing everyone's attention to one point while the real attack came from another direction. Most of all, Clint warned them to keep their wits when and if the shooting started. Panic-stricken men are more dangerous to their friends than they are to their foes in combat.

The Gunsmith also met with Ben Watson and Timber Barton to discuss their situation. Plans for building defenses, prolonged strategies and possible offensives against Jarrad were considered. Ben and Timber supplied information, but both men clearly looked to Clint to assume the role of leader until the crisis was over.

Clint was amazed and amused by the situation. He'd never been a soldier, yet they regarded him as a military commander. The Gunsmith had never cared much for giving orders and he liked taking them even less. He'd taken charge of Jackass Gap simply because he had to. Someone had to give the scared and weary miners leadership and shake them out of their stupor and back to the world of the living.

The Gunsmith had completed his fourth day at Jackass Gap. His schedule had been hectic and most of the work was monotonous, a bit tiresome and mentally exhausting. He entered his shack and hoped to get as much sleep as possible between midnight and dawn.

Clint prepared to unbuckle his gunbelt when he heard a woman scream. He immediately bolted out the door, his Colt already drawn and ready for action. A few of the miners had wives and children in the camp, but the nearness of the woman's voice suggested it belonged to his closest neighbor—Carolyn Gray Fox.

He headed for the girl's shack, moving in a low crouch as he ran. His eyes and ears were keenly alert for any dangers lurking in the shadows. Carolyn was as tough and brave as any man and Clint doubted that she'd scream without one hell of a good reason. He was surprised to see the sentry on duty at the center of the camp merely shrug and ignore the girl's cry.

"It's nothin', Adams," the guard informed him. "Go back to sleep."

"What the hell do you mean?" Clint snapped.

"Carolyn has nightmares sometimes," the sentry replied in a bored voice. "Ever since young Tom Watson went off and never come back. You get used to her hollerin' after a while."

The Gunsmith shook his head. He could never get used

to hearing a woman wail in anguish the way Carolyn cried at that moment. He hurried to her door and pounded a fist on it.

"Carolyn!" he called. "It's me. Clint. Are you all right?"

Almost a full minute passed before the door opened and Carolyn Gray Fox's face appeared. Her loveliness was marred by the redness of her eyes and the sheen of hastily brushed tears on her cheeks. She seemed totally different than she had before—disoriented, frightened and vulnerable.

"I'm all right, Clint," she said weakly. "Just a dream. I'm sorry. . . ."

"Don't be." He gave her a reassuring smile. Her hurt, emotionally shaken expression attracted Clint to Carolyn as much as her courage and intelligence had before.

"Well," she smiled feebly. "I'm embarrassed. . . ."

"Everybody gets rattled by a nightmare that seems real at the time," Clint said, managing to slip across the threshold to enter the shack. "Want to talk about it?"

"Not really," Carolyn replied. "Thanks anyway. . . ."

Even in the unlit room, Clint saw that Carolyn had hastily pulled on a man's shirt which she held together with one hand. That was *all* she had on. The hem of the shirttails reached her upper thighs and Clint tried not to stare at the long shapely legs displayed by the short garment. He also felt hot, lustful desire for this brave, beautiful lady.

"It might help to talk," Clint said, moving closer. "You really shouldn't be alone after having a bad dream."

"There's nothing that can be done about it," she said. "Nightmares aren't made of flesh and blood. You can't fight them."

"Not with a gun or knife," Clint admitted, placing a hand on her cheek. "But you can still fight them by trying to understand what causes the dream."

"I know its cause," Carolyn told him. Her voice was firm, but she didn't move away from him. "And nothing will change it."

"Then try to take your mind off the source," he suggested.

Clint took her in his arms and crushed his lips against hers. Carolyn stiffened in surprise, then returned his kiss. The Gunsmith pulled her closer and she raised her hands to his chest and tried to push him away. He didn't retreat, holding her fast and inserting his tongue in her mouth.

Carolyn didn't make any further attempts to resist. Her arms snaked around his neck as she kissed him harder. Fiery passion poured from her mouth. Carolyn's tongue groped along his teeth while her hands gripped his shirt to secure a handle, pressing them closer together.

The Gunsmith wanted her. He hadn't wanted a woman so badly for a long time. Clint gathered her up in his arms and carried her across the room. Carolyn's body was light and firmly muscled, but the soft warm flesh of her naked thighs was smooth and feminine in his palm. The flames of desire burned in his loins as he quickly located the girl's bed among the shadows.

He placed Carolyn on the cot and fell to one knee before her. His hands caressed her legs and thighs, pushing the hem of her shirt higher. Clint's lips replaced his fingers to kiss her upper thighs. He licked at her warm flesh until his tongue found the musky portal of love. Carolyn gasped and slowly parted her legs.

They quickly stripped off their clothing. Carolyn lay on her back and Clint mounted her. The girl took his throbbing, hard member and steered it into her womanhood. Both moaned with pleasure as he slid inside. The

Gunsmith tried to control his urgency and rotated his hips to gradually work himself deeper.

"Oh, Clint!" she gasped, clawing into his back with her nails.

He increased the tempo until her body convulsed in pleasure. Carolyn's wonderful, strong legs wrapped around his torso, locking themselves at the ankles to press against the small of his back. She began to buck and tremble as an orgasm coursed through her. Clint thrust harder, faster; he gritted his teeth as she ground herself against him and rode Clint to a second pinnacle of joy. At last, he released his seed and they journeyed to paradise together.

Both man and woman breathed heavily as they lay spent and exhausted on the thin mattress. Clint held the girl tenderly, kissing her neck, face and lips.

"That was wonderful, Clint," she whispered. "I don't know if it was right or wrong, but it was still wonderful."

"It was for me too," he told her, meaning every word.

"But I'm afraid you'll have to go now," she said sadly.

"If that's what you want," Clint agreed reluctantly.

"It's the way it must be," Carolyn insisted. "My fiancé hasn't been dead long, Clint. It isn't proper."

"Yeah," he said as he rose and reached for his clothing. "Your memories of him must still be pretty strong and painful."

"Worse than painful. They're a torment."

The harsh tone of her voice startled Clint. He could see little of her face in the shadows, but her clear green eyes seemed to harden as she stared up at the ceiling.

"The dream," Carolyn whispered. "It's always the same."

"Do you want to talk about it?" Clint asked, no longer certain he wanted to hear about the nightmare.

"I can see Tom," she began in a strained voice. "I see

him lying on the ground. He's hurt and he can't move, but he's still alive. There are two men standing over him. They look like a pair of shadows. I can't see their faces, but one of them has a knife in his hand.''

Clint felt a cold shiver crawl up his spine.

''Then the two men kneel beside Tom,'' she continued, still staring up at the ceiling. ''He tries to struggle, but they've tied him down. He can't move as they unbutton his trousers and begin to pull down his pants. The man with the knife . . .''

''Jesus!'' Clint rasped.

''I know what I see in those dreams is what happened to Tom,'' she declared. ''They cut—''

Her voice broke and Clint felt the bed tremble. He placed a hand on her shoulder. ''Honey,'' he said softly. ''It's just a dream. You can't—''

''I know it's real, Clint,'' she said in a choked voice.

''Carolyn . . .''

''You have to go now, Clint,'' she insisted.

He almost protested, but decided it would do no good. Clint pulled on his clothes and buckled on his gunbelt. The Gunsmith wanted to say something to Carolyn, but what? Tell her that dreams aren't reality and the nightmares merely expressed her own fears about her fiancé's fate and it didn't mean Tom had actually been tortured by his assailants? Should he assure her that Tom would be avenged or that, for a while, he'd be there to supply her need for a man?

None of this would make any difference or give her any comfort. So Clint Adams left the shack without saying another word. As he stepped outside, he shivered, recalling Carolyn's nightmare and her conviction that she'd witnessed Tom Watson's ordeal.

It's not possible, he thought. *She couldn't know. For the love of God, don't let it be possible. . . .*

TWENTY-FOUR

The Gunsmith returned to his shack and unbuckled his gunbelt to hang it on the headboard of his bed. Then he pulled off his boots and lay down, not bothering to remove the rest of his clothes. He hadn't realized how exhausted he was until he closed his eyes and immediately fell into a deep, sound sleep.

A gunshot awoke him. Excited shouts followed and another shot mingled with the voices. Clint rolled out of the bed, snatching his pistol from its holster. He bolted to the door in his stocking feet and peered outside to see the pink and gold dawn splashed across the early morning sky. He also saw a miner sprawled face down on the ground. Other men dashed for cover as a third shot erupted.

Clint saw the muzzle flash of a rifle located among the rocks beyond the camp. The Gunsmith noticed Timber Barton crouched beside another shack, a Winchester in his hands. Taking a deep breath, Clint dashed out the door and ran to the other man's position.

"Are we under attack or is this just sniper fire?" Clint asked, recalling what Ben had said about Jarrad's previous acts of harassment.

"Appears to be snipers," Timber replied. "I figure two, maybe three fellers out there among the rocks."

"How many of our people have been hit?"

"One so far."

"Do you think any more of the enemy are stationed at another position?"

"They've never tried to hit us with a crossfire in the past and there ain't been no shots fired at us from any other direction this time neither," Timber answered. "I'd say this is probably just standard Jarrad harassment."

"Yeah," Clint muttered. "They already harassed one man to death. Let's not take any chances. Have enough men at their posts to cover the surrounding area, but arrange a concentration of fire on the snipers' main position. I want them pinned down as well as possible long enough for me to circle around from the south to their location."

"You gonna try to take 'em by yourself?" Timber frowned.

"One man can move faster and quieter than a group," the Gunsmith replied. "You get the men ready and I'll get my boots on."

Three minutes later, the defenders of Jackass Gap were carrying out Clint's orders. Half a dozen men fired their rifles at the snipers' hiding place while the others covered the surrounding area. Clint Adams, wearing boots, gunbelt and his Springfield carbine in hand, darted to the south end of the campsite and headed for the rocks.

Hoping the concentration of rifle fire would keep the snipers preoccupied, Clint ran to the stony walls, painfully aware of the lack of cover between the camp and the boulders. However, no bullets were fired in his direction and he reached the rocks undetected . . . at least, he hoped so.

Scrambling behind the boulders, trying to move as silently and swiftly as possible, Clint circled around the approximate position of the snipers. He seized a scrawny

cottonwood to haul himself up to the lip of a rock formation and found himself on top of a wide, flat-topped
boulder—where one of the enemy riflemen happened to
be stationed.

The sniper, lying prone on the rock with his rifle aimed
at the campsite, heard the Gunsmith's boots land behind
him. Clint—just as surprised as the gunman—saw the
enemy half turn to face him. With a cry of alarm, the
gunman tried to roll around to snap off a shot at Clint.
Firing from the hip, Clint's Springfield roared and a .45
caliber slug tore into the soft tissue under the sniper's jaw.
The bullet then tunneled through the roof of the man's
mouth before it sizzled into his brain and popped off the
top of his skull.

The shot immediately alerted the sniper's partners.
Two figures stationed among the boulders turned to confront Clint. The Gunsmith threw himself flat beside the
body of the man he'd killed. A rifle slug burned air inches
above Clint's head as he hastily worked the lever of his
Springfield to chamber another round. A second bullet
chipped stone from the rock a foot from Clint's face. A
fragment tugged at the brim of Clint's stetson as he swung
his carbine toward the nearest sniper.

The fellow was still working the lever of his Winchester
when Clint blasted a .45 into his chest. The force of the big
slug smashed the sniper backward to fall against a boulder
before he slumped in a lifeless lump. The third man aimed
his rifle and squeezed the trigger—to discover his gun was
out of ammunition.

Panic-stricken, the last member of the sniper team
threw his rifle aside and clumsily scrambled across the
rocks, desperately trying to escape from the Gunsmith.
Clint chambered a fresh round and carefully aimed his
Springfield at the fleeing figure. He lined up the sights of
his carbine and squeezed the trigger. His bullet went right

where he wanted it, a direct hit in the back of the sniper's right thigh. The man screamed and half turned before he plunged over the edge of a boulder to crash to the ground below.

Still watching for other opponents, Clint worked the lever of his carbine once more before he surreptitiously moved to the fallen man's position. He found the sniper easily enough because the fellow wasn't going anywhere. He'd fallen headfirst into another boulder. The Gunsmith felt his stomach turn as he gazed down at the man's body. His skull had been split open and the contents had splattered the corpse with assorted gore.

Damn, Clint thought. He'd wanted to take at least one of them alive. Still, it was better to have three dead enemies than to be a victim himself. He shouted at the defenders within the camp and waited for them to cease fire. When he was certain he could enter Jackass Gap without getting his head blown off by his own men, Clint returned to the campsite and reported the outcome of the gun battle to the others.

"Looks like Jarrad's men lost another round," Timber Barton remarked.

"He can afford to lose more men than we can," Clint replied. "And when he figures out he lost those five guys sent to ambush you yesterday and today's sniper team, he'll probably change tactics."

"You think he'll try to attack the town?" Carolyn inquired.

Clint shrugged. "I don't claim to be able to read minds, but we'd better prepare for it just in case."

"Your supplies and ammunition have helped, Clint," Ben Watson said. "But we're still too low on food and cartridges to either wait Jarrad out or fight him on a large-scale level."

"That's a fact, Clint," Timber agreed. "Just shooting

back at those snipers exhausted almost a third of our ammunition.''

"Then we have to get more," the Gunsmith declared. "I'll need three volunteers to join me."

"What are you planning to do, Clint?" Ben asked.

"We're going to take a buckboard to the nearest town and get more supplies," Clint replied. "And we'll have to be ready to fight our way through anything Jarrad throws at us on the way."

TWENTY-FIVE

To everyone's astonished relief, Clint and the men with him—Timber Barton and the two miners named Jeff Paxon and Cole Summers—drove their buckboard from Jackass Gap to the next town without encountering any of Jarrad's hired killers along the way. Hardly a word had been spoken during the tense journey since no one wanted to take the chance of being distracted by conversation until they reached their objective.

"I can't believe we made it to Papa's Town without no trouble." Timber sighed, breaking the long silence as he expressed what every man in the wagon felt.

"You figure maybe Jarrad's pulling in his horns since he found out we can fight back?" Jeff Paxon asked the Gunsmith.

"I wouldn't count on it," Clint warned. "He probably guessed we wouldn't dare make a move outside of camp after the snipers hit us. When he figures out that his boys won't be coming back . . . well, our trip back to Jackass Gap might not be as peaceful."

"Reckon we'll worry about that later," Timber remarked as they approached the collection of crude adobe huts known as Papa's Town.

Clint looked at the shabby little buildings and shook his

117

head with dismay. "Are you sure we can buy supplies here?"

"Sure can," Cole Summers assured him. "Papa Nelstrum and his family make their living by selling supplies to mining communities and travelers. Kind of a family tradition with them."

"Yeah," Clint commented dryly. "And it sounds like the family are all a little crazy too."

"Maybe they are," Timber agreed. "But like I told you before, this isn't exactly a town because nobody lives here but old Papa Nelstrum and his kin. That's the way they want it. The family keeps to themselves and they make it clear that outsiders are welcome only as customers. They don't want anybody to stay. Papa makes the laws here and everybody has to obey them as long as they're in town."

No sooner had Timber finished speaking than three large, formidable figures with full beards emerged from one of the adobe shacks. All were powerfully built and not one of them was less than six foot two. Although dressed in patched, old clothing, the trio possessed a unique form of simple dignity.

Two of the trio held shotguns. They appeared to be young men, but the thick beards that covered their faces made it difficult to guess their ages. The third man, however, was clearly their senior by many years. He was as big as his younger companions with a flowing white beard and a mane of snowy hair which framed his stern, wrinkled face. He casually placed a hand on the butt of a pistol that jutted from a holster in a cross-draw position.

"Howdy, Papa," Timber Barton said. "Been a while since we've been to your town. How've you been?"

"Life has been good for me and mine," the old man replied in a deep, strong and surprisingly gentle voice. "We ask little of the Lord and have been blessed with more than we expected. That is His way."

"We need to buy supplies, Papa," Timber explained. "Food, barrels of water, ammunition."

Papa nodded. "We have done business before, Mr. Barton, and you have always been a good man." His eyes fell upon Clint Adams. "This one is not from your camp, is he?"

"Not exactly," Timber began. "But he's a friend. Name's Clint Adams and he wishes you and your clan no harm, Papa Nelstrum."

Papa's gaze remained on Clint as he spoke. "Since you are new to my town, I will tell you of our laws, Mr. Adams. You may buy what you need. If you have little money, gold or silver, we might be willing to trade, but we will not give credit to those we do not know. It is sad yet true that trust is a thing that must be earned in matters of business."

"That's reasonable," the Gunsmith replied.

"We do not welcome outsiders to spend the night because we are a hermitlike people and our ways are not like your own. We will sell you whiskey, but we ask that you do not drink it until you leave. You may smoke tobacco here, but not the Mexican herb that makes one like a drunkard. My sons and I have wives and children here. You will leave them be for we do not want them taught your ways. We believe our traditions bring them closer to the Lord."

"I understand," Clint told him, deciding the man was neither crazy nor a fanatic. A religious extremist is convinced his faith is the only true one and generally tries to force his notions on others. This did not apply to Papa Nelstrum who said "we believe" instead of "we are right." He didn't insist "you will believe," merely "allow us to have our beliefs in private."

"Also," Papa continued, "we must ask that you leave your guns here with your wagon and that you do not put them on again until you have left this town. A wise man does not encourage armed strangers into his home."

Clint didn't like this condition. "We have enemies, Papa Nelstrum," he explained. "Enemies who have already killed many of our friends . . ."

"Matthew twenty-four, verse six: *'And ye shall hear of wars and rumours of wars . . .'* That is the way of the world." Papa nodded. "That is why we have made our own world here. We'll thank you to keep your wars out of our town, Mr. Adams."

"But you have guns," Clint noticed.

"Indeed," Papa admitted. "How else can we protect our home? I must insist our laws be obeyed."

"If our enemies arrive, they may not be willing to oblige to your conditions," the Gunsmith warned.

"Then that will be their misfortune," Papa declared as he raised a hand over head.

Suddenly, numerous rifle barrels jutted from doorways and windows in every building in Papa's Town. The old man waved his hand and the guns withdrew inside the houses.

"If anyone is to be killed in our home," Papa stated, "we shall do the killing. Now, put up your guns and come forward or go in peace."

"Feller sure has a way with words, don't he?" Timber grinned at Clint.

"Yeah," Clint replied, unbuckling his gunbelt. "You might say he's downright disarming."

Timber and the two miners headed for one of the shacks. Clint, unfamiliar with the town, followed. He was surprised to discover the interior of the little building was lined with wall shelves and filled with display cases, all stocked with weapons, ammunition and tools. A dour bearded man waited on them behind a counter. He remained polite but said little as they selected and bought several dozen boxes of shells for various weapons in several different calibers.

A visit to another shack revealed that it contained a storehouse of canned foods and bags of grain, coffee, flour and beans. Clint was impressed by the assortment of merchandise available in Papa's Town and he noticed that the prices were reasonable.

Carrying plenty of supplies, the four men stepped from the store to see five barrels of water had already been loaded onto the wagon. Surprised, Clint turned to Timber who smiled.

"Papa never charges us for water," he explained. "The old feller says rain comes outta the sky from God and it's meant for all livin' things so he don't figure it's right to put a price on it. The barrels themselves will cost us a nickel each. We even get a refund if'n we return the barrels in one piece."

"Papa's my kind of businessman," Clint commented.

They headed for the buckboard, but suddenly froze in their tracks when they saw five newcomers who stood on the opposite side of the street. Timber, Paxon and Summers could only guess who the men were; the Gunsmith, however, immediately recognized Baltimore Smith and Parako, which left no doubt that all five men were on Alfred Jarrad's payroll.

TWENTY-SIX

Baltimore Smith and Parako were as surprised to encounter the Gunsmith as Clint was to see them in Papa's
Town. Parako recovered from the shock and quickly
swung his hand to his hip for a pistol, but Papa Nelstrum
had obviously met the group as well and forced them to
remove their weapons before entering the town. Parako's
hand clenched into an angry fist by his empty holster.

"What are you doing with these men, Adams?" Smith
demanded as he marched toward Clint and his friends.

"I'm about to help them load their wagon," the
Gunsmith replied, lowering his burden of coffee bags and
tinned food to the ground.

"Are these some of Jarrad's men?" Timber Barton
asked, dumping his supplies as well. "I've been itchin'
for a chance to get my hands on one of 'em. . . ."

"Shut up, fat man," Smith snapped, his eyes still
locked on Clint. "Don't tell me you were stupid enough to
quit workin' for Jarrad so you could side with these
dumbshit miners!"

"Smart-mouth bastard!" Timber growled. "I'll make
you eat them words along with your friggin' teeth!"

"Take it easy, Timber," Clint urged. He turned to
Smith. "Look, why don't we talk about this? You're not

122

stupid, Smith. You have to realize Jarrad's actions are irrational.''

"So are yours, Adams.'' The easterner grinned. "You're downright suicidal! You side with these miners and you're as good as dead.''

''A lot of men are already dead,'' Clint told him. "And lately your side has been losing a lot more than ours. How about calling a truce and see if we can't talk some sense into Jarrad?''

"Sense?'' Smith chuckled. "We're gonna collect a share of a silver mine, Adams. The biggest mother lode to be discovered in more than a decade. You think I'm going to turn that down? What do you think I should do, Adams? Go back to the goddamn slums in Baltimore? Not when all we have to do is stomp out a few dirty mules like this fat man—''

"Damn you!'' Timber snarled. "You come and try to stomp me, you maggot-eatin' pig!''

"You will take your violence out of our town!'' Papa Nelstrum demanded as he and his two shotgun-toting sons approached.

"Right!'' Parako shouted. He glared at Clint. "Let's get outta this Christers' paradise and you and me can see who is really top dog with a gun!''

"I don't need no gun with the likes of you!'' Timber bellowed, rolling up his sleeves. "You fellers are mighty brave when you're shootin' at folks from the cover of rocks, but let's see if'n you've got the sand to take on a man on equal terms!''

"You boys stand back,'' Baltimore Smith told his men as he tossed aside his derby and stripped off his vest to reveal the empty shoulder holster under his left armpit. "The fat man wants a fight, so I'll give it to him!''

"There'll be no killing in our town!'' Papa declared.

"Ain't gonna kill him, Papa," Timber stated. "But I'm surely gonna give this city slicker the beatin' of his young life!"

"Timber . . ." Clint began, but the tough, ex-lumberjack had already launched himself at Baltimore Smith.

The two men seemed pretty evenly matched. Smith was taller than Timber, but the miner was thicker and more muscular than his opponent. Timber raised his fists like a pugilist while Smith calmly hooked his thumbs under the buckle of his brass-studded belt.

Clint's eyes widened. "Timber! Don't!"

But he was too late to warn his friend. Smith suddenly yanked off his belt and lashed it across Timber's face. The miner cried out and half pivoted from the blow, his left cheek slashed and bloodied by the brass studs that had whipped into his face.

Baltimore Smith stepped forward and flailed his deadly belt weapon across Timber's head and shoulders. Timber ducked low and tried to raise his arms to protect his head. Smith quickly moved in and slammed a knee into his opponent's battered face. Timber crashed to the ground.

"That's enough!" Clint declared, moving forward. Parako and the others did likewise.

The eruption of a shotgun blast immediately caused everyone to halt abruptly. One of Papa's sons had fired into the sky to warn all present that the situation had gone as far as the Nelstrums would allow.

Timber, however, rose to his feet and shook his scarlet-dripping head. He saw Baltimore Smith casually wrap his vicious belt around his right fist while he smiled at Timber. The sturdy, stubborn Timber Barton grunted something under his breath and again charged forward, still determined to teach Smith a lesson.

Baltimore Smith raised his right fist, displaying the gleaming metal studs on the belt. Timber jerked to the right, ready to dodge the improvised cestus, but Smith's move had been a feint. He hit Timber with a solid left hook to the jaw. The miner stumbled from the unexpected blow and Smith moved in to ram a fast uppercut with the belt-draped right to Timber's solar plexus. He hit Timber again and the other man gasped and fell forward to land on his hands and knees.

"Stop!" Papa shouted.

Smith ignored him as he stepped behind his dazed opponent. He swung his fist again, smashing the brass-studded leather into the base of Timber's skull. Barton fell on his face and didn't get up.

Clint rushed to his fallen friend and knelt beside him while Baltimore Smith stepped back to rejoin his companions. Nelstrum glared at Smith.

"I told you to stop," he declared.

"Had to be sure the fat man wouldn't come at me again," Smith shrugged.

Clint placed two fingers at the side of Timber's neck, trying to find a pulse although the crushed occipital bone at the back of the man's head told him the effort was folly.

"He's dead," Clint announced as he rose to his feet and stared at Baltimore Smith. "You and I have something to settle now, Smith."

The easterner nodded. "If that's how you want it, Adams."

"You'll settle with me first, Gunsmith!" Parako declared.

"I've heard enough from you, boy!" Clint snapped. "If you're so eager to get killed, I'm ready to oblige you!"

"There has been enough killing and talk of killing!" Papa Nelstrum stated. "Mr. Adams, you and your friends have your supplies. You will please take them and the body of Mr. Barton, and leave."

He turned to his shotgun guards and thrust a finger at
Smith, Parako and the other three gunmen. Nelstrum's
sons immediately trained their weapons on the five startled men.

"We will keep you here for exactly one hour," Papa
stated. "Long enough for Mr. Adams to return to Jackass
Gap. If you plan to resume your war, that will be your
choice, but if another life is to be taken in our home, a
Nelstrum will pull the trigger!"

"You crazy old—" Parako began, but the yawning
barrels of two shotguns convinced him to shut up.

Papa turned to Clint Adams. "I am sorry about Mr.
Barton and I hope his soul has been received and blessed
by the Almighty Love of God in Heaven," he said.
"And I hope you and your friends at Jackass Gap can
come to an understanding with Mr. Jarrad. Isaiah two,
verse four: *'and they shall beat their swords into plow-
shares, and their spears into pruninghooks: nation shall
not lift up sword against nation, neither shall they learn
war any more.'* "

"I just tried that a minute ago," the Gunsmith replied
grimly. "Guess we'll just have to follow the advice from
Leviticus twenty-four, verse twenty."

With that he began to help Paxon and Summers load
Timber Barton's corpse onto the buckboard. Papa
Nelstrum had been surprised by Clint's knowledge of the
Scriptures; he knew the verse Clint had mentioned.

Breach for breach, eye for eye, tooth for tooth . . .

TWENTY-SEVEN

The citizens of Jackass Gap were stunned and grieved by the death of Timber Barton. Clint Adams addressed the crowd that formed around the buckboard as several men carried the dead body of their trusted friend from the wagon.

"I know you're all feeling a lot of hurt right now," he said. "So am I, believe me. So am I. But Timber wouldn't want us to mourn him, he'd want us to keep fighting just as he'd fought until the end.

"We've got plenty of supplies and ammunition and we'll be able to fight Jarrad better than ever now," he continued. "Jarrad and his men have already taken too much from us to let him win now and—"

Clint suddenly saw an unexpected yet familiar face among the congregation. Darlene Farrell looked back at him with a sly smile.

"—I give you my word," he concluded. "Jarrad won't win."

Clint then worked his way through the crowd to reach Darlene. He took her by the arm and steered her away from the others. The girl journalist whispered, "That was quite a speech, Clint. What do you plan to do about—"

"What the hell are you doing here?" he demanded. "Oh, shit! Never mind. You're still hunting down a big story for your readers, right?"

"And do I ever have one now!" Darlene grinned. "When I heard the rumor about a struggle between this mining town and Jarrad's ranch for control of a silver mine, I never dreamed you'd be involved as well."

"I seem to have a talent for getting myself in the middle of the worst kinds of trouble," Clint said dryly. "Something we have in common."

"Can't you see the human drama here?" Darlene continued. "Good against evil, right against wrong—"

"And real people dying on both sides."

"But *you're* the big story, Clint." Her eyes shone as she spoke. "You're the modern day Sir Lancelot who rescues helpless women from savages and champions the downtrodden people of this town against Alfred Jarrad and his army of professional killers. You're going to be a new American hero, Clint."

"Darlene," Clint said with a sigh. "I'm already as famous as I can stand. I don't want any more fame and recognition."

"Don't overdo the humility angle," she advised as she got out her notepad. "No one will believe it."

"All right," Clint said. "Write this down."

"Ready, Clint."

"Being a living legend is a pain in the ass," he declared. "And you can quote me."

He left Darlene with her mouth hanging open and headed for Ben Watson's shack. Ben was seated at his cluttered desk, poring over a map with a number of technical drawings on it that were meaningless to the Gunsmith.

"I'm sorry about Timber," Clint began. "I know you and he were close friends."

"Like you said, Clint," Ben replied in a slightly strained voice, "the best memorial we can give him is to see to it Jarrad doesn't win."

"Are you working on something to achieve that goal?" the Gunsmith inquired.

Ben nodded. "This is a map of the mine." He pointed at the chart on his desk. "Now, in the past, we know Jarrad has had men stationed on the opposite side of the mountain, but he's never put anyone at the mouth of the mine because that's too close to Jackass Gap."

"Do you think he has anyone positioned on the blind side of the mountain now?" Clint asked, trying to figure out what all the lines and circles meant on Ben's map.

"Maybe he does and maybe he doesn't," Ben replied. "But one thing is certain—if he plans to launch a major offensive against us, he'll want as much reconnaissance as possible to learn how we've set up our defenses."

"Sounds reasonable," Clint agreed. "And he'd probably put men in a position where they could get the best view possible in order to obtain the information."

"You've got it, Clint." Ben smiled. "The best site would naturally be at the mine itself."

"So your idea is to beat him to it and set up a strong defense at the mine before he can get a team there?"

"Right," Ben confirmed. "If Jarrad's people show up, our men will open fire and we'll hear it and come to their assistance. What do you think?"

"I'd say it's a damn good idea," Clint told him, "providing we can supply our men with ample cover so Jarrad's killers can't just pick them off with sniper fire from the rocks above."

"They'll have the best cover possible, Clint," Ben declared. "The mountain itself. We'll post men at the mouth of the mine. Nothing short of a pound of dynamite could get to them then."

"What if Jarrad gives his men dynamite just for that very reason?"

"He won't," Ben answered. "Because if he blows up that entrance, he'll seal the mine and bury it along with our men. He doesn't want to lose that silver and he knows from past experience he isn't a good enough miner to get to it if he destroys our tunnel. Besides, even if he'd be willing to do that, his men damn sure wouldn't take the chance and wind up having to wait months for the silver to be uncovered again."

"Good point." Clint nodded. "So let's round up our best sharpshooters just in case some of Jarrad's boys are up there and get a team together to post at the mine."

"Only one problem." Ben knitted his brow. "There's a smaller tunnel that serves as an emergency escape exit located on the side of the the mountain, here." He pointed at a square-shaped drawing that didn't look like a mountain or a tunnel to Clint. "We'll have to seal it off to be certain Jarrad's men don't sneak through and ambush our people from within the mine."

"Okay," the Gunsmith said. "Who is your best powder man? We'll take him along to blow the side entrance shut."

"I'm the best explosives expert here."

"You can't go," Clint stated. "That crippled leg of yours would be too much of a handicap on the rocks if we have to move fast. Besides, with Timber gone, you're the only leader these folks will have left if anything happens to me up there."

"You don't have to go."

"I should go with them to coordinate the post set up and to escort the demolitions man in case of trouble. After all, I have the best background in handling gunfights. So, who will the powder man be?"

"Well, next to myself, the best choice would probably be Sean McKenna."

Clint frowned. "The jackass killer?"

"I know." Ben sighed. "But he is a good man when it comes to explosives."

"Okay." Clint shrugged. "Just make sure there's some whiskey left when I get back. I have a feeling I'll be ready for a couple good stiff drinks after this is over."

TWENTY-EIGHT

Six men cautiously made their way to the mountain Alfred Jarrad had christened the Hill of Hope. The lack of sniper fire from the stony giant earned a sigh of relief from every man in the team when they reached the mouth of the mine.

The mine's entrance seemed sinister to Clint Adams. Thick oak beams had been built to support the surrounding rock mass, creating an unnatural doorway in the side of the mountain. The blackness within the tunnel was ominous, like the gateway into Hell. Clint recalled Jarrad's story about Sylvia's experience as a little girl inside such a black pit. His flesh crawled at the mental image it created. He didn't envy the four men who'd be stationed at the mine for the next forty-eight hours.

To the miners, of course, the main fear was a possible encounter with Jarrad's killers. They'd made their living by digging in that mine and it held no unspeakable terrors for them. Their only worry was whether the rest of the camp would be able to come to their rescue quickly enough if there was shooting.

The four volunteers moved to the mouth of the mine and dumped their backpacks which contained food, water, extra ammunition and plenty of blankets. The smoke from a campfire in the daylight, and its glow after dark could

alert Jarrad's men of their position, so they'd have to do
without.

After the guards set up at the mine, Clint and McKenna
moved around the side of the mountain. Travel was more
difficult due to clusters of rocks and boulders before they
reached the smaller cavity of the mine's emergency exit.
Clint was stunned by the difference in the size of the
opening. The main tunnel was used to haul ore cars and
mules inside as well as men while the side door was only
large enough for men to crawl through in case of an
accident inside the mine.

McKenna had been surprisingly eager to accept the
mission, which led Clint to suspect he may have misjudged the Irishman. McKenna barely said a word as they
moved along the Hill of Hope to the smaller tunnel. He
remained silent while he unslung a musette bag from his
shoulder and began to remove sticks of dynamite from it.

Although it was McKenna who handled the task of
inserting blasting caps into the dynamite and crimping the
sticks as he prepared them, Clint was the nervous one. The
Gunsmith didn't like being around dynamite—which can
be highly unstable depending on its age, how it has been
stored and the weather. The nitroglycerine in the wood
pulp can settle to one side if the sticks haven't been turned
from time to time; it can leak in warm weather or freeze in
cold. Even an expert could make a critical and fatal
mistake with dynamite.

"I'm about ready to light the fuse," McKenna announced as he rose and dusted off his trousers, calmly
looking down at the explosive bundle at his feet.

"Then we'd better get out of here," Clint said. They
couldn't get far enough away soon enough to suit him.

"The fuse burns about a foot a minute and we've got
two feet of fuse so—" McKenna's eyes suddenly wid-

ened, staring at something behind Clint as he clawed at his holstered sidearm.

The Gunsmith pivoted, drawing his Colt in a single, swift motion, but he saw nothing to explain the alarm on McKenna's face. He was still looking at the rocks for some sort of threat when he heard McKenna's footsteps behind him.

"Over there," the Irishman said, pointing at a group of boulders.

"What?" Clint asked, gazing at the rocks.

Then he heard something slice through the air behind his left ear an instant before a hard object crashed into his skull. Brilliant, painful light exploded before his eyes and he felt his knees buckle. Everything suddenly vanished and he fell into empty black oblivion.

TWENTY-NINE

The worst thing about being knocked unconscious is regaining one's senses afterward. The first thing Clint became aware of was the throbbing pain at the back of his head. He stifled a groan as a glimmer of reason warned that to announce his return to consciousness might not be wise.

Clint had been knocked out before and he was familiar with the aftermath. His head would hurt like a first-class hangover and his vision would be blurred. He'd be tempted to just lie where he was and drift off to sleep, but he knew this could be disastrous.

Exerting willpower over the demands of flesh, Clint forced his eyelids to part. Darkness still surrounded him. This jolted the cobwebs from his mind. *Oh, God!* he thought. *Have I been blinded?* His hand groped for the comfort of his modified Colt on his hip, only to find the holster empty.

His skin felt clammy and the air around him was motionless and cold. A sense of claustrophobia gripped him as he felt the rocky surface beneath him. Then he heard something sizzle, the sound echoing from somewhere deep within the shadows.

The fuse.

"Holy shit!" Clint gasped, swallowing a mouthful of stale air.

The Gunsmith's head seemed to whirl around on his neck as he forced himself to stand. Lights popped before his eyes and a wave of nausea rose up from his stomach. Clint nearly blacked out again, but the terrifying reality of the situation added fuel to his determination to stay on his feet.

Even dazed and groggy, Clint put together the puzzle about what had happened and where he must be. After McKenna had slugged him, the Irishman had dragged Clint inside the mine—which explained the darkness, the stale, clammy air, and the sensation of constricted surroundings.

Clint's eyes adjusted to the darkness and he could make out a few vague shapes among the shadows. A ribbon of light extended from one direction. The sound of the burning fuse reminded him he had less than two minutes to either get clear of the explosives or find the dynamite and extinguish its fuse. Thanks to the echo within the tunnel and his own dulled senses, Clint couldn't tell which direction the sizzle came from, so he had no choice except to head for the light and hope it either led him out of the mine or to the dynamite in time to deactivate it.

He staggered forward as fast as he could, nearly tripping over the iron rails of an ore-car track. Clint slapped a palm against a rock wall as he ran, half bracing himself and half propelling himself onward.

Gradually, the light increased and he saw the rails at his feet and the wooden supports mounted against the narrow confines of the mine. Clint kept moving, his legs wobbling beneath him as he continued his desperate, stumbling dash for survival. He no longer heard the fuse sizzle, only his own ragged breathing and the hammering sound of a pulse behind his ear.

Then the world exploded. A horrendous roar filled the mine, the sheer force of the blast pitching Clint forward into a tumble that carried him painfully into a natural wall of stone. Smoke and dust billowed through the cavern and the sound of crashing rock and timber penetrated the ringing within his aching ears.

Clint rose slowly, glad to be alive and even more grateful that he hadn't been buried under tons of debris. The explosion had come from behind and the patch of light remained before him. Clint was heading for the main entrance, toward freedom and life. He began to stagger on to the glorious exit from Hell. . . .

The scream of metal against metal, of gears too long without oil, turned his attention once more in the direction of the explosion. A large, blocklike object suddenly hurtled forward like a freight train from Hades. Clint gasped in horror when an ore car, filled with hundreds of pounds of rocks, a monster of metal and stone, rocketed straight for him along the iron rails.

Clint ran, fear adding new speed and strength to his weary legs. The explosion had propelled the ore car with incredible force and it was gaining on him rapidly. He tried to find an area by the rock walls with enough room to avoid being crushed by the pursuing car. Nothing! He had to keep running toward the light. The car seemed to increase momentum as it chased Clint. The Gunsmith felt as if he was experiencing the ultimate nightmare—being pursued by an inhuman, indestructible adversary in a dark, claustrophobic cave.

Then Clint tripped on a beam that had fallen across the tracks. As he scrambled to his feet he realized that the fallen beam had been the only thing between him and certain death—for in front of him now was a huge crater, which he stared into, struggling to keep his balance—and his sanity. The pit was roughly nine feet wide and at least sixty feet deep. Behind him, the ore car continued to roar closer. . . .

The Gunsmith leaped forward, extending his body full length, desperately trying to reach the opposite side of the pit. If he missed and fell, the car would come crashing down on him even if he survived the sixty-foot drop to the bottom of the hole of death.

His hands and arms slapped against the rough surface of the edge of the pit. Clint's belly slammed against the rocky wall of the crater's interior, his boots wildly kicking for a foothold. Then he heard the ore car hit the fallen timber and topple over the edge of the pit. The crash of more than a ton of iron and rock below threatened to jar Clint's grip loose. A cloud of dust rose up to assault his mouth, nose and eyes.

Then, almost before he knew it had happened, Clint's grip slipped and he began to fall.

Something caught his left boot and he felt his knee connect painfully with the rock wall of the pit. His flailing hands seized an object mounted against the side of the crater. To Clint's amazement, he'd managed to grab a ladder that had been set inside the pit. He clung to the rungs and tried to gasp for breath, but the billows of rock dust poured into his nostrils and threatened to gag him.

"After surviving all this shit," he muttered, coughing hard, "I'm not about to choke to death . . ."

Then the rung under his boots snapped and he felt his body plunge once more. Clint's grip on the ladder prevented the fall, although the sudden strain on his shoulders nearly yanked his arms loose. A foot found another rung and he hastily climbed the ancient, half-rotted ladder.

A rung broke off in his right hand and he managed to seize the frame of the ladder with his left before he lost his balance. Nearly to the top, he reached for the edge of the pit. Suddenly the entire ladder groaned and began to sway to the side, taking Clint with it. Wood cracked below as the base of the ladder began to give way under his weight. Once more, the Gunsmith began to fall.

"Jesus!" a voice exclaimed as strong hands grabbed Clint's shirt front and arms.

Two men quickly hauled him over the top of the pit while the ladder collapsed and crashed into the black hole. Clint gazed into the faces of the four miners who'd been stationed at the mouth of the mine.

"I told you I heard somebody movin' in here," one of the men declared. "But I didn't figure it was you, Mr. Adams."

"What the hell are you doin' in here anyway?" another miner asked.

"Staying alive," the Gunsmith replied feebly.

THIRTY

"Saints preserve me!" a voice shouted as footfalls rushed toward the mouth of the mine. "Adams insisted on takin' the dynamite inside o' the mine and I fear the poor man has gone and blown himself to Kingdom Come!"

"McKenna!" Clint snarled under his breath.

"Did you hear me, boys?" the Irishman cried as he jogged toward the entrance of the tunnel. "I said, Adams went and—"

McKenna's eyes bulged and his jaw dropped like it had been filled with lead shot when he saw the Gunsmith push his way past the other four men to charge forward in a murderous lunge for McKenna's throat.

A few seconds before, Clint would have sworn he was too exhausted and emotionally rattled to do anything but sit and rest. He would have been certain the only things he wanted were to see sunlight and breathe clean, fresh air beyond the tomblike interior of the mine. But McKenna's voice had sparked a violent, almost maniacal urge that sent a new charge of fearsome strength into his weary body.

Clint attacked like an animal, snarling with rage as he leaped upon the treacherous Irishman and closed his fingers around McKenna's throat. The lunge carried both

140

men hurtling into the side of an iron bin which contained an assortment of mining tools.

McKenna's left hand pried at the Gunsmith's grip on his throat while his right reached for Clint's face, trying to gouge an eye with his thumb. Clint jerked his head to avoid the attack and promptly rammed the back of McKenna's skull into the side of the bin. Still holding the man by the throat with his left hand, Clint clenched his right into a fist and hit McKenna in the face with all his might.

The Irishman fell heavily on his back, blood oozing from a split lip. His hand reached for the gun on his hip before Clint stamped on his wrist. McKenna howled in pain and Clint kicked the revolver out of his reach.

Suddenly, McKenna seized Clint's ankle and pulled him off balance. The Gunsmith toppled to the ground, but managed to roll on a shoulder and quickly rose. McKenna had also gotten to his feet. He'd also reached into the tool bin and extracted a pickax with a long hickory handle and a wicked blade with iron points jutting from both sides.

The other four miners watched dumbfounded as McKenna attacked, slashing the tool at Clint's head. The Gunsmith ducked under the whirling blade and managed to dodge McKenna's next swing, which drove one of the pick points into the ground. Clint punched the Irishman in the face, the blow knocking him backward, but also serving to jar the blade of the pick free from the ground.

Clint jumped to the tool bin as McKenna raised his pick and charged again. He swung the weapon in a fast overhead stroke. The Gunsmith whirled, holding a shovel in his fists. The shaft of Clint's tool met the handle of the pick below the blade, stopping the Irishman's attack.

The Gunsmith raised a foot and rammed it into McKenna's belly as one might try to kick in a door. The big man staggered backward, but kept his balance. Clint lashed out with the shovel, smashing the flat of the blade into a set of fingers holding the handle of the pick. McKenna cried out and withdrew his shattered hand. Clint swung the shovel again and batted the pick out of his opponent's grasp.

Before the startled Irishman could recover from his surprise and pain, Clint stepped forward and slashed the shovel into his adversary's midsection, driving the edge of the blade into McKenna's diaphragm. The big man gasped and fell to his knees in a groaning heap.

Fortunately, Clint's anger subsided and he regained control of his temper before he could use the shovel to shatter his opponent's skull. Clint tossed the tool aside and reached down to rip the musette bag from McKenna's shoulder. Opening it, he found his .45 Colt revolver.

"You're lucky I got this back, you son of a bitch," he told the dazed Irishman.

"Mr. Adams?" one of the four miners began, obviously wondering if Clint or McKenna, or both, had gone insane. "Would you mind explaining what the hell this is all about?"

"McKenna here is the one who has some explaining to do," the Gunsmith stated. "Start talking, you oversized leprechaun, before I decide to shoot you in both kneecaps, drag you into the mine and dump your ass into that goddamn pit!"

"Jarrad—" the Irishman began, rubbing his battered diaphragm as he fought to regain his breath. "Jarrad contacted me a couple months ago when he heard we was mining at his Hill of Hope. Once a week, every Friday night about midnight, I'd sneak out of camp and meet with one of his men. Told them how things were going and whether we'd found silver that week or not. Told them about the mother lode and later told them about our defenses and how we had guards set up, how our supplies were holdin' out . . . everything . . ."

"You son of a two-cent whore!" one of the miners spat.

"Why'd you try to kill me?" Clint demanded.

"Last night I was on guard duty when one of Jarrad's men, a feller named Parako, showed up. He called softly to me and when I sneaked off to talk with him, he told me Jarrad wanted you dead. You've killed a lot of Jarrad's boys and some of the rest of his men have lost their nerve lately and run out on him 'cause they didn't want to tangle with the Gunsmith. When I saw a chance to kill you today—"

McKenna suddenly turned to gaze up at the four miners. "Don't you see?" he said in a pleading voice. "I did it to save us all! Jarrad's gonna kill everybody in Jackass Gap if we don't pull out. . . ."

"Then why didn't you just advise everybody to leave and get out yourself?" Clint asked coldly. "You're on Jarrad's payroll, McKenna. How many pieces of silver does a fella get these days for betraying his friends?"

"No!" McKenna wailed. "I—"

"I'm going to take this traitor back to town," Clint declared. "Let's see what everybody back there thinks we should do with him."

"If anybody suggests hanging the bastard," a miner remarked, "I'll cast my vote right now in favor of the notion."

Three other voices echoed, "Aye!"

THIRTY-ONE

The citizens of Jackass Gap voted on how to deal with
Sean McKenna. Twenty-three of the twenty-five men,
women and children in the community were in favor of
hanging the Irishman. The other two wanted to see him
tied to two mules and pulled apart like a butterfly in the
hands of a vicious kid.

Darlene Farrell gasped in horror when the townsfolk
seized McKenna and tied his arms behind his back. The
Irishman tried to struggle and received a brutal thrashing
from a dozen men and two angry women for his efforts.

"Clint!" Darlene cried as she dashed to where the
Gunsmith calmly watched the proceedings. "You can't
let them do this!"

"Why not?" he replied with a shrug. "It's their town."

"But these people have become a lynch mob!"

"I noticed," Clint agreed.

"That man should receive a trial."

"Everybody agrees he's guilty," Clint told her.
"McKenna even confessed to the crime. The verdict is in
and the bastard was found guilty."

"But this is so cold-blooded."

"These folks aren't the least bit cold-blooded," Clint
corrected. "Their blood is boiling over. They've lost

friends and family because of McKenna's treachery. I couldn't stop them if I tried.''

"And you won't try, will you?'' She glared at him.

"Okay,'' the Gunsmith said with a sigh. "Hey,'' he called out in a conversational tone, "don't hang that man.''

None of the angry, snarling mob heard him.

"There,'' Clint told Darlene. "I tried. Happy now?''

"I'm not going to just stand by and—''

"Oh, really?'' He smiled without humor. "Are you going to get your camera and take a picture of McKenna dangling by a rope from a tree, just like you photographed Parako standing beside the men he gunned down back at Jarrad's ranch?''

The girl's head snapped back as though Clint had struck her. Before she could think of a reply to his accusation, the Gunsmith continued.

"Or will you write a newspaper story about how the terrible people of Jackass Gap took the law into their own hands and strung up a son of a bitch who'd betrayed them? Will your article mention the fact that there isn't any duly appointed officer of the law in this county? Shit! This isn't even a county!

"What kind of trial do you think Jarrad gave the people he had killed in order to try to drive these folks out? Where was the law when these folks were starving or when sniper bullets were pouring into it? What about their rights, Darlene? Why don't you tell your readers the truth? If a man has money and power he can break any damn law he wants until somebody stops him. Sometimes it isn't the law who does it—it's people . . . Americans who want their most basic freedoms such as life, liberty and the pursuit of happiness . . . the very things Jarrad would take from them.

"Tell your readers that justice doesn't always come in

the formal trappings of a courtroom. Tell them that a traitor deserves a rope and a would-be warlord deserves to have his petty dictatorship and private armies destroyed. Tell them the truth for a change. Maybe somebody will listen.''

Suddenly, the crowd fell silent. They stood around the base of a cottonwood, the only one in Jackass Gap large enough to be called a tree. Sean McKenna dangled from one of the branches, suspended by a rope attached to his neck. The man's body convulsed and twisted like a giant fish at the end of a line. His feet kicked and slashed at the air for almost a full minute before his muscles stopped responding and his broken neck convinced the rest of his body that he was dead.

THIRTY-TWO

Someone cut down Sean McKenna's corpse and several men lowered it into a blanket on the ground by the base of the tree. Another blanket was placed over the body, carefully covering his discolored face. Then six men solemnly gathered up the bundle and carried it outside of town where four more men with picks and shovels were already digging a grave.

Clint watched the somber-faced pallbearers march their burden to the gravesite. He noticed most of the townsfolk had lowered their heads and a few crossed themselves. The Gunsmith shook his head, thinking of the paradoxical behavior of the human race. A few minutes ago the people of Jackass Gap were fighting each other for the honor of putting a noose over McKenna's neck, but now that he was dead, the Irishman received all the formal rituals and customary gestures of sorrow associated with funerals.

Darlene was another example of the contradictions of human nature. The girl who'd photographed Parako with his trophies had thrown up and retreated to her room after she'd witnessed the execution of Sean McKenna—who had been a back-stabbing son of a bitch that deserved the necktie party held in his honor. Perhaps this was because Parako had killed two men in a so-called gunfight, a duel

147

which presented the illusion of fair play. This appealed to the girl's sense of local color in the wild, untamed West. McKenna's execution, however, had been simple, direct and brutal. There isn't any way to glamorize a hanging.

"Clint?" a feminine voice called softly.

He turned to face Carolyn Gray Fox. "Yes?"

"Ben wants to talk to you about the defenses for the town," she explained.

"Okay," he nodded. As they walked to Ben Watson's shack, Clint asked Carolyn, "How do you feel about today's execution?"

"I'm glad we killed the son of a bitch."

"Who says women aren't logical or honest?" Clint smiled.

"Oh"—Carolyn laughed—"you must have talked to that newspaper woman. She asked me how I felt about all the violence and killing involved in this mess. She wanted a woman's point of view for her story."

"What did you tell her?"

"I said I didn't like violence or killing, but I felt better when we were killing Jarrad's men than when it was the other way around." Carolyn shrugged. "Poor kid nearly fainted when I told her I'd killed a couple of the bastards myself."

"Maybe she'll turn you into a living legend too." Clint grinned. "Killer Carolyn of Jackass Gap."

The girl rolled her eyes and groaned in response.

THIRTY-THREE

Benjamin Franklin Watson welcomed Clint and Carolyn. He gave them both a cup of freshly brewed coffee and waited until they were seated before sinking into a chair behind his desk.

"I know we talked about our defense measures earlier today," he began. "But that was before we knew about McKenna's treachery."

"Do you think that changes things much?" Carolyn inquired.

"It might," the Gunsmith said. "McKenna said that he'd been contacting a representative from Jarrad's camp every Friday night. That means he hadn't been able to give them any information—until last night when Parako talked to him and said Jarrad wanted me killed."

"The question is," Ben said, "how much did he tell Parako about our defenses?"

"And how much did that dumb trigger-happy kid remember when he reported back to Jarrad?"

"Come on, Clint . . ." Ben sighed with exasperation.

"All right." The Gunsmith nodded. "You're right, of course. McKenna may have jeopardized our security with his big mouth—if we continue with the same tactics we've used so far."

Ben wrinkled his brow. "So you suggest we change our defenses?"

"No," Clint declared. "I propose we do the unexpected and launch an *offensive* against Jarrad."

Ben Watson leaned back in his chair and stared at Clint as though he questioned the Gunsmith's sanity. Carolyn, however, leaned forward, eager to hear Clint's plan.

"But you told us the Big J is an armed fortress surrounded with guards posted at the wire," Ben said, gesturing with open palms as if pleading with Clint to reconsider.

"That's true. But it's also true that McKenna said Parako told him that a number of Jarrad's men had decided the risks were too great and they hightailed out of the Big J."

"After all," Carolyn said, "up until a few days ago Jarrad hadn't lost a single man. We've killed about ten of them now. Imagine how shocked those polecats are. The wolves went after the sheep and the sheep turned on them and won!"

"Exactly," the Gunsmith agreed. "I told you before that most of Jarrad's men aren't professional gunmen. They're just garbage-can scum who figured this would be an easy way to make a lot of money without taking much of a risk. They didn't think we'd be able to put up a decent fight."

"But attacking Jarrad's ranch . . ." Ben began, still opposed to the idea.

"Look," Clint explained, "if Parako relayed anything about us to Jarrad, it's that we've been improving our defenses here at the campsite. Now, Parako and Smith were both at Papa's Town and they've certainly told Jarrad that we've now got plenty of supplies and ammunition. My guess is Jarrad will realize he can't hope to starve us out and he can't risk sending sniper teams anymore because we wiped out the last one.''

"You mean *you* wiped them out," Carolyn corrected.

"A moot point. What matters is that Jarrad will now be concentrating on a full-scale attack, hoping to massacre everyone at Jackass Gap. He won't expect us to hit him first.''

"If you're right," Ben said, ''that means we'd better act fast unless we want to trade lead with his killers in a full-scale battle here.''

"Your men would be slaughtered if that happened," Clint told him. "Jarrad's forces only have a couple real professionals, but every man on his team is a killer who won't hesitate when it comes to pumping bullets into someone for a profit. Most of them are probably better with a gun and more experienced fighters than the majority of our people.''

"But we'll still be faced with the same problem if we attack Jarrad's ranch," Ben declared. "They'll be slaughtered at the Big J instead of here.''

"Not if we rely on cunning instead of fire power," the Gunsmith replied. "We have to come up with a plan that will allow us to penetrate Jarrad's defenses and won't require our men to be better gunmen than our opponents.''

"I trust you have such a plan in mind?" Ben asked.

"Well"—Clint shrugged—"let's say I'm working on it.''

THIRTY-FOUR

The Gunsmith entered his shack, his mind busy with the strategy he was trying to develop for the assault on Alfred Jarrad's ranch. He wasn't expecting company, but he found Darlene Farrell waiting for him.

She was seated on his bed—naked.

"I want to talk to you," she explained with a smile.

"Well," Clint replied, trying to mask his surprise, "you sure know how to get a fella's attention."

He crossed the room to the bed and unbuckled his gunbelt. "As a matter of fact, I wanted to see you too."

"You're seeing quite a lot of me right now," Darlene purred, running her fingers along his inner thigh. "Aren't you?"

"Maybe right now isn't the best time to talk," he commented, unbuttoning his shirt.

"Why?" she asked as she began to unfasten Clint's trousers. "Is there something else you'd rather be doing?"

"Hardly," he assured her. "It's just we might feel more like talking a little later on."

"I want to apologize for my behavior earlier today," Darlene told him, pulling his pants down to his ankles. "That man they hanged today was largely responsible for

152

everything that's happened to these people and I really shouldn't judge them too harshly for how they dealt with him.''

"Darlene?"

"Yes, dear?"

"Will you let me take my boots off now?"

"Oh," she replied as he sat beside her and tugged off his boots before stripping away the last of his clothing.

"Anyway," Darlene concluded. "I wanted you to know I think what you said was right . . . that is, most of it.''

"I'm glad to hear that," he assured her as he gently eased her back onto the mattress.

"But your attitude about journalists is still awfully hostile," she complained, but her arms embraced his neck as she spoke.

"I don't seem hostile, do I?" Clint inquired, lowering his face to kiss her breasts.

"Oh, not now," she moaned as he nibbled on her skin.

"Not now?" Clint raised his head to stare at her with surprise.

"You don't seem hostile now," Darlene explained. "I didn't mean that I didn't want you to—"

"You had me worried for a minute."

He put his hand between her legs and gently caressed the girl. Darlene sighed with pleasure and began to playfully bite his left shoulder. Clint gradually mounted her and Darlene helped him slide his swollen manhood into her chamber of love.

"Oh, that's goood!" she moaned as he slowly worked himself deeper.

Clint increased the speed and penetration of his thrusts. Darlene arched her back to receive him and gasped with pleasure. She squirmed against the mattress, getting herself closer to his pelvis. Clint followed her motion, rotating his hips accordingly. Then he pumped faster and harder.

Darlene grabbed his hair and pulled forcibly as a convulsion of pleasure sent her into a near frenzy. The girl cried out and Clint hoped no one would hear her because it sounded as if she was in agony instead of sensuous ecstasy. Wouldn't it be wonderful if somebody decided to check on the girl's screams? To be interrupted by a couple of well-meaning, overzealous miners would be embarrassing as hell . . . and what if Carolyn happened to be present?

Before Darlene could cry out again, Clint clamped his lips over her mouth to silence her and rode the girl to a shuddering climax. He blasted his seed into her at the same moment and they came to a wild, exhausting orgasm together. Delightfully spent, they lay snuggling close together and breathing hard after their enthusiastic lovemaking.

"You're one hell of a man, Clint Adams," Darlene sighed contentedly.

The Gunsmith kissed her forehead. "I'm glad we've patched up our former differences."

"Me, too," Darlene agreed. "Oh, what did you want to talk to me about?"

"Well," Clint began awkwardly, "I have a favor to ask."

"What?" she frowned.

"I want to borrow your horse and buggy," he replied.

THIRTY-FIVE

An hour later, Clint and Darlene met with Ben Watson and Carolyn Gray Fox in Watson's quarters. Ben gazed down at the map he'd drawn according to information the Gunsmith had given him of the Big J ranch. Clint admitted he'd only seen the entire spread once and he couldn't swear to accuracy about distances or positions of guard stations along the perimeters of Jarrad's property.

"You say the guard teams are stationed a mile apart?" Ben asked, glancing up at Clint.

"That's the way it was set up before I left," the Gunsmith confirmed. "My guess is Jarrad has probably reduced the guard units because he's lost some manpower and he probably decided we're going to remain on the defensive."

"Yeah," Carolyn commented dryly. "But the fact that he had so much security set up to begin with suggests he has considered the possibility we might try an organized attack on the spread."

"I didn't say this would be easy," Clint stated. "But if our plan works, we should be able to take the place with a minimum of bloodshed."

"*If* your plan works." Ben nodded. "It still seems awfully risky to me."

"I think it's worth a try," Carolyn said. "I wouldn't be going otherwise."

"Are we going to argue about that again?" Ben looked at her sharply.

"No," she smiled. "Because I've already made up my mind. I'm going. Clint, you agree that I should be part of the team, right?"

"I don't want to," the Gunsmith said, "but I can't find any logical reason to exclude you. Besides, you have one damn good argument in your favor—you're a woman."

"Then I'm going too," Darlene announced.

"Sorry." Clint shook his head. "No way."

"Why can Carolyn go and I can't?"

"Because you've never used a gun in your life and this is a damn poor time to try to give you a fast lesson in survival," Clint answered bluntly. "Carolyn has proven she can take care of herself so she qualifies."

"But you promised me a story," Darlene insisted.

"If any of us come back," the Gunsmith began, "we'll give you all the details. You'll have your story. If we don't come back, you'll probably never get to write it anyway."

"Meaning?" Darlene asked, certain she didn't really want to know the answer.

"If the plan fails," Clint explained, "Jarrad wins. There won't be enough men left here to defend Jackass Gap. I reckon within twenty-four hours Jarrad's men will respond by hitting this town and killing everyone in it."

"Including me," Darlene said woodenly.

"Welcome to the West," the Gunsmith told her.

THIRTY-SIX

As twilight fell, Ben Watson asked for volunteers for the mission. Nearly every man in Jackass Gap wanted to go. Clint Adams talked to each man individually, trying to select the best for the job. He finally chose ten of them.

Ben Watson, past his prime and crippled, would remain in Jackass Gap with the others and concentrate on keeping the town defenses at the highest level possible—a token gesture, largely to comfort those who stayed behind.

Clint searched through the gear in his wagon and found a black stetson and denim shirt and a dark pair of Levi's that would serve as night clothing. He fed and watered Duke and brushed the gelding's rich black coat.

The Gunsmith returned to his quarters, carrying his dark clothing under an arm. He placed the bundle on his bed and opened one of his saddlebags to get the final item for the mission. Clint extracted his .22 New Line Colt from the bag. A diminutive pistol, the New Line was an ideal belly gun, highly concealable yet lethal at close range. He often carried the little holdout gun under his shirt, tucked in his belt. Taking on Jarrad's army of killers would require every trick the Gunsmith had. The New Line would go with him.

He unbuckled his gunbelt and began to change his clothes when someone knocked on the door. He invited

the visitor to enter. The door opened and Carolyn Gray
Fox stepped across the threshold. She smiled thinly and
closed the door.

Clint couldn't help noticing the girl's wonderful
breasts that strained the fabric of her denim shirt or the
beautiful shape of her legs, displayed by her tight Levi's.
He recalled the thrill of her kiss and her passionate lovemaking. Clint hoped she hadn't just stopped by to wish
him good luck, but he didn't jump to any conclusions or
ask why she'd paid him a visit. Carolyn would tell him
soon enough.

"One or both of us might be killed tonight," she began.
"This might be our last chance to be together."

Clint nodded. *Wishes do come true.*

They made love with fiery desperation because Carolyn's observations were all too accurate. Each tried to
make it the best, most fulfilling experience they'd ever
known. Carolyn, like Clint, was not selfish and tried to
bring him as much pleasure as possible instead of seeking
it only for herself.

And when they were finished and lay together in a
tender embrace, Clint came to a startling conclusion.
Carolyn was more than a wonderful sex partner and a
beautiful woman. She was brave and intelligent and noble. He admired her personality even more than her beauty
and her virtues even more than her prowess in bed.

What Clint felt frightened him because he'd vowed
never to fall in love again. . . .

THIRTY-SEVEN

Phil Bonner wearily rolled a cigarette as he gazed beyond the barbed wire fence and wondered how long he'd put up with Alfred Jarrad's bullshit.

When he'd been recruited to drive off cattle rustlers, Bonner had been delighted and amused. Hell, he had fled to Nevada because there was a five hundred dollar price on his head in California. Bonner was wanted for armed robbery, assaulting a deputy marshal and cattle rustling. The irony of the offer stunned the petty outlaw. He planned to play along and pick up a couple hundred from Jarrad until he got a chance to throw in with the rustlers and help them steal enough of the rancher's prize cattle to earn a position of honor and respect in the gang.

Then he learned the truth about his employer and the Hill of Hope. Bonner was stunned. All he had to do was help starve out some dumb miners at Jackass Gap and throw a little lead in their direction once in a while to keep them good and scared. Then the miners would move out and Jarrad would move in to claim the silver. Bonner and the others on the crafty rancher's payroll would receive enough silver to allow them to wear linen shirts, drink French wines and screw high-class whores for at least a year.

But Bonner didn't figure he'd have to be standing

goddamn guard duty every night or that he'd find himself
up against a man like the Gunsmith. He'd always heard
that Clint Adams was probably the fastest gunfighter in
the West. Maybe Bill Hickok could have taken Adams
. . . maybe. Bonner had also heard Adams was a do-
gooder. He'd never believed it until the Gunsmith decided
to join those damn miners at Jackass Gap.

Well, fast gun or not, even Adams wouldn't be a match
for all the men working for Alfred Jarrad when they finally
quit playing around with those tunnel diggers and hit
Jackass Gap like Sherman done to Atlanta. Old Man
Jarrad said that time was coming pretty quick too.
Couldn't be soon enough for Phil Bonner. Hell, he was
sick of marching around on guard duty as if he was in the
goddamn Army.

Bonner had just reached for a match when he saw
something move beyond the wire. The shape of a horse
pulling a wagon of some sort appeared from the shadows.
He spat out his cigarette and turned to the two men who
crouched by the campfire.

"Leon! Waco!" he snapped. "Somebody's comin'!"

The two men, a pair of small-time hootowls like Bonner, quickly scrambled away from the fire and gathered up
their rifles. Bonner slipped the retaining thong from the
hammer of his holstered Hopkins & Allen revolver so he
could pull it out of leather. The trio held their breath and
watched the rig's gradual approach.

"Aw, shit!" Bonner muttered when he recognized the
eastern-style horse and buggy. "That must be the same
nosy female newspaper snooper who showed up here a
few days ago."

"You sure, Phil?" Leon asked, still gripping his Henry
carbine, ready for trouble.

"Who the hell else would be ridin' around in a damn
fool contraption like that?" Bonner replied gruffly.

"What's she doin' out here at this hour?" the outlaw known only as Waco wondered. "Must be past midnight by now."

"Hell, I don't know," Bonner snorted. "Girl's probably crazy anyways. Well, the old man run her off once before so we'd better do likewise. . . ."

"Hold up, Phil." Leon grinned. "I seen that girl and she's a real looker. Why don't we have us some fun with her 'afore we send her runnin' back East to her fancy newspaper office?"

"Sure would give her somethin' to write about." Waco chuckled.

"Aw, I don't know," Bonner replied. "I never forced myself on no female . . . 'cept my wife and I run out on her 'cause I got tired of havin' to fight her all the time."

"Don't worry none, Phil." Leon smiled. "She won't have no fight left in her after I get through with the snotty little bitch."

The horse and buggy rode up to the fence. The trio stared at the woman who sat alone in the rig. She was one handsome female, sure enough.

"Hey," Leon remarked, "that ain't the same girl."

"Who cares?" Waco growled. "She's a looker too . . . and she's alone."

"Howdy, ma'am," Bonner greeted. "You get yourself lost or somethin'?"

"Something like that," Carolyn Gray Fox confirmed as she held the reins in one hand and placed the other on a blanket draped over her lap. "I wonder if you could help me?"

"We'll purely try," Waco said.

"This is the Big J ranch?" she inquired.

"Sure is, little lady," Leon replied. "You got some kinda business with Mr. Jarrad?"

Clint Adams swung his head and right arm out from

under the belly of the carriage, his left hand and both legs still clinging to the mainshaft under the rig. He aimed his .45 Colt at the trio and cocked the hammer to get their attention.

"You bet your lives we've got business with him," the Gunsmith announced.

Carolyn quickly produced a Remington .44 pistol from under the blanket and aimed it at the startled gunmen. "And unless you fellers want to lose that bet," she told them, "you'd better drop those guns."

"Aw, shit," Bonner moaned.

The trio dropped their guns.

A few minutes later, all three sentries had been securely bound and gagged. "That's the last of the sentries along the wire," Clint said, checking the knots. "Glad that's over. Riding *under* a carriage isn't the most comfortable form of transportation."

"It was your idea," Carolyn grinned. "And a good one. We caught every one of them off guard and we haven't had to fire a single shot."

"Yeah"—Clint nodded—"so far."

He struck a match and held it overhead, waving the flame slowly before the breeze blew it out. In the distance, another fire of a match replied to the signal. Less than a minute passed before ten men on horseback approached them—the rest of the group from Jackass Gap.

"Your plan worked without a hitch, Clint," Carolyn said. "We've put almost half of Jarrad's men out of action and nobody's been hurt."

"Don't get overconfident," the Gunsmith warned. "We've still got some pretty hard odds to take on."

"I know," she said softly.

"Look, Carolyn," he began, touching her arm. "I don't want anything to happen to you. Okay?"

"The feeling is mutual, Clint," she assured him.

"When this is over," the Gunsmith said, "I think you and I ought to have a talk."

THIRTY-EIGHT

One of the miners cut the barbed wire between two fence posts. Jeff Paxon rode his sorrel stallion through the opening to enter the sacred domain of the Big J ranch. Cole Summers followed, riding a piebald gelding and leading Duke by the reins. The Gunsmith quickly mounted his big black Arabian and patted Duke's neck.

"All right," Clint said, his voice just above a whisper, "everybody knows what to do. If you have any questions, better ask them now."

"How do we find the bunkhouses where them other fellers will be?" a voice inquired dully.

"Hell," another miner growled. "Clint told us all we have to do is go 'round the back of the big house and we'll find everything laid out like a little town."

"What if those guards we tied up manage to get loose?" a third voice asked.

"We took their guns and horses," Clint replied. "Pretty unlikely they'll try anything even if they do get free, and if everything goes smoothly we should be finished before any of them can manage to untie themselves."

There were no more questions.

"Okay," the Gunsmith said. "Cole, Jeff and I are going to leave now. The rest of you wait three minutes and

then move. Everything has gone fine so far. If nobody
loses his head and we keep having luck on our side, we
might be able to wrap this up without anybody getting
hurt.''

"If anybody does get hurt,'' a grizzled miner began, "I
hope it's that son of a bitch what beat Timber to death.''

"Baltimore Smith.'' Clint nodded. 'I told him he'd
have to settle with me for that . . . and I'm a man of my
word.''

Clint, Paxon and Summers rode toward the front gate.
Five of Jarrad's hired gunmen were posted at the main
entrance. They looked at the three advancing figures on
horseback with surprise, but since Clint and the miners
were inside the perimeters of the spread, they assumed the
trio were fellow members of Jarrad's private army.

"What are you fellers doing at our post?'' one of the
sentries asked as he laid the barrel of a Winchester across
the crook of his elbow and folded his arms over it.

"We're here to relieve you of duty,'' Clint Adams
announced as he drew his modified Colt revolver.

Before any of the startled sentries could decide to make
a move for their guns, Summers and Paxon produced
pistols and pointed them at the five gunslingers. The
sentries' rifles fell to the ground and they raised empty
hands over their head.

When the rest of Clint's team arrived, the gate was
standing open and the five sentries had been disarmed,
bound and gagged. The miners grinned with wolfish satisfaction as they dismounted. The second phase of the
Gunsmith's plan had gone as smoothly as the first. Clint
realized, however, that the third step was the most
dangerous.

"You'll find several bunkhouses behind the house,'' he
whispered to his crew. "Each has a six-man capacity, but

a lot of those guys were on guard duty so most of the buildings will only have a couple men inside and most of them will probably be asleep. Don't shoot unless you have to, but don't hesitate if a fella goes for a weapon. Shoot to kill."

"Don't worry," Carolyn assured him.

"I know *you* won't hesitate." He rolled his eyes in mock despair, although in fact Carolyn was the only member of the team he knew he could rely on if fighting broke out.

"After you get the guys inside the bunkhouses to surrender," he continued, "be sure to get them *outside* so they can't get their hands on a weapon stashed away in the room. Whoever covers the prisoners while the others check out the remaining houses, don't let *anything* distract you. Remember, if you drop your guard, one of these fellas can turn on you quicker than a rattlesnake.

"You'll also find a cantina, a stable and a shop back there. The men who work in those places aren't gunmen and they probably aren't outlaws either. I don't think they'll put up a fight, but don't assume they're harmless."

"What about the main house?" Carolyn asked. "Are you still determined to go in there alone?"

"I've been in there before and I'll be able to find my way around in the dark easier alone. Besides, Parako and Smith are probably there and I'm the only one who can handle those two if it comes to a showdown."

Carolyn prepared to say something, then shrugged, aware that Clint had made up his mind.

"Okay," Clint said with a sigh. "Let's go. Good Luck."

THIRTY-NINE

Clint located the French windows to Alfred Jarrad's study and slipped the blade of a stockman's pocket knife between them to jimmy the latch. He pried one of the windows open and entered the house. The Gunsmith gave his eyes time to adjust to the darkness within before he crossed to the door.

He opened it and peered into an empty and dark hallway. Clint shivered. Somehow, the shadows and walls reminded him of the silver mine. Slowly, Clint moved forward, drawing his pistol.

The Gunsmith walked through the hallway on the balls of his feet, his Colt held in front of him like a divining rod. Although the corridor was dark, he noticed a strip of light extending from the bottom of a closed door.

As he approached, Clint was surprised to hear a man softly singing beyond the door. The voice was a rich, full tenor and the song was a Spanish ballad. The Gunsmith wasn't fluent enough to understand it all, but he caught enough words like *amor* and *amor mio* to recognize it as a romantic ballad.

He reached the door and knelt low to peer through the keyhole. The singer sat in an armchair in a room which appeared to be a parlor. Clint didn't associate the gentle Spanish lyrics or the sensitive singing voice with the man in the room. He could only see the back of the fellow's head, but he was certain the straight black hair belonged to Parako.

Everybody has a good quality or two, he thought as he cautiously turned the doorknob. Too bad Parako had chosen to cultivate his abilities as a gunfighter instead of his voice. The Gunsmith slowly eased the door open. The hinges creaked slightly. To Clint, it sounded like a rusty train wheel squeaking on an iron rail, but Parako was too involved in his song of love to notice.

Holding his breath, Clint stepped forward. Parako still sat with his back to the door, singing to an imaginary *señorita* and gesturing flamboyantly with one hand while the other held a long-stemmed glass, half filled with dark red wine. Clint continued to creep forward, expecting the young gunhawk to turn and discover him at any second.

Parako failed to sense the presence of the Gunsmith and continued to sing until Clint whacked the barrel of his Colt across the gunman's skull. The wine glass fell to the floor and shattered. Parako sighed as though suddenly bored with his music and collapsed unconscious in the chair.

"That really wasn't meant as a criticism of your singing," the Gunsmith whispered.

"Drop your gun," a woman's voice ordered, "or I'll criticize you to Hell!"

Clint didn't drop his Colt, but he raised his arms slowly and turned to face Sylvia Jarrad who stood in the doorway—a lovely, ghostlike figure in a white robe, with a .36 caliber Navy Colt cap-and-ball pistol in her hands.

"I told you to drop your gun, Clint," she said in a hard, flat voice, her eyes blazing like violet fire in her pale face.

"You do move quietly, don't you?" he remarked.

"And I shoot well enough to kill you from this distance," Sylvia warned.

"Why would you want to kill me?" he asked.

"Father said you're working against us now," she replied grimly. "You've betrayed me in more ways than one, Clint. Don't think I won't shoot you now."

"Sylvia," he began, "do you know what your father has been doing with the men he's hired? Do you realize he's been having people killed to try to seize control of the silver mine at the mountain he calls the Hill of Hope?"

Sylvia stiffened and her eyes widened in an expression Clint couldn't read for certain—surprise, horror, disbelief, perhaps all three.

"He swore he'd never go back there," she whispered. "He promised none of us would ever have to go back there again."

"That was before a group of miners found silver there," Clint explained. "Your father has no legal claim to that silver, but he's killed to try to get it."

"Nothing but evil exists in the Hill of Hope," Sylvia hissed. "I know. I know that better than anyone."

"Your father feels otherwise."

"That's a lie!" she snapped, suddenly thumbing back the hammer of her Navy Colt.

"Then why am I here, Sylvia?" he demanded. "If I'm a cattle rustler, I wouldn't be inside this house. Do you think I'm a burglar?"

"I don't know," she admitted, confused and upset by what she'd heard.

"Sylvia," Clint said softly, "I don't think you want to shoot me. I'm going to lower my arms and put my gun in its holster to show I mean you no harm."

"No!" she said sharply. "Drop it!"

"I can't," he replied, slowly lowering his arms. "There may still be men in this house who will try to kill me so I can't allow you to disarm me."

"You came here to kill my father!" Sylvia accused, her hands trembling.

Clint looked at the wobbling pistol in her grasp and tried
to swallow his fear. Nervous hands are more apt to pull a
trigger by accident.

"No, Sylvia," he assured her. "Your father has to be
stopped, but I don't want to kill him. Maybe if you and I
both talk to him, we can convince him he's wrong."

"Clint . . ." she said weakly, apparently because she
didn't know what else to say.

The Gunsmith lowered his left hand to his side as he
shoved his Colt into its holster. "Let's go see your father,
Sylvia."

She uncocked her pistol and dropped her arms to her
side, pointing the gun at the floor. "All right, Clint,"
Sylvia agreed. "But I want your word that you'll let my
father tell his side and you won't hurt him."

"You have my word," Clint told her.

"Father is upstairs," she said. "Follow me."

FORTY

Clint and Sylvia left the parlor and headed for the staircase when they heard gunshots erupt outside the house. Sylvia, who led the way because she was familiar with the house and moved better in the dark than the Gunsmith, abruptly turned to face him.

"That's coming from the bunkhouses," she declared. "What's happening out there?"

"The people I came with are trying to subdue your father's collection of killers. We wanted to do that without bloodshed, but I guess the gunmen don't want to oblige."

She thought for a moment. "We'd better find my father as fast as possible."

Clint couldn't argue with that. He followed her pale white form up the stairs. Sylvia still moved with remarkable grace and silence. She seemed to float up the stairs while the Gunsmith hurried to keep pace with her.

At the head of the stairs, they saw flickering light dancing along a wall in the next corridor. Clint slipped past Sylvia, his Colt already in his fist before she could protest. The figure of Baltimore Smith appeared in the hallway, holding his S&W pistol in one hand and a lantern in the other.

"Freeze, Smith!" Clint ordered. "Or I'll cure your insomnia for good!"

171

The eastern gunman stiffened and apparently considered the odds of pivoting and firing at Clint. He wisely decided against it and dropped his weapon.

"No tricks, Smith," the Gunsmith warned. "Place that lamp on the floor and then move away from it."

"You'll never get out of this house alive, Adams," Smith said tensely, but he obeyed the Gunsmith's instructions.

"That'll make two of us, then," Clint warned. "Now, step toward the wall and face it. Keep your hands high. I've seen you use that killer belt of yours. Reach for it and you're dead."

"You're holding all the aces," Smith remarked, still following orders. "For *now*."

"Sylvia," Clint began. "Get your father and bring him here. I'll keep the Baltimore bastard covered."

The girl didn't utter a word or even nod. She simply vanished into the darkness of the corridor. Clint watched Smith carefully as he kicked the S&W further down the hall.

"How about a deal, Adams?" Smith suggested, still facing the wall.

"Sure," Clint replied. "You shut your mouth and maybe I won't kill you."

"Hell, Adams," the easterner snorted. "This is just business. You shouldn't take it personal."

"I'll personally make you dead if—"

"Adams!"

Clint turned to see Parako on the top landing. The young gunhawk's pistol was aimed at Clint's stomach. The Gunsmith mentally cursed himself for not tying up Parako or at least disarming him before he left the pistol-man unconscious in the parlor.

"Kill him, Parako!" Smith shouted.

"If he fires that gun, Smith," Clint declared, his Colt

still pointed at the easterner, "you'll die too. As for you, Parako, you'd better make sure you kill me with the first shot because if I manage to live long enough, I'll take you both with me."

"I'll only need one shot." Parako grinned as he mounted the stairs, his weapon still trained on Clint. "But I'm gonna give you a chance, Gunsmith!"

"Don't be a fool—" Smith snapped.

"Shut up, you greenhorn!" Parako snarled. He stepped onto the head of the stairs and stood opposite Clint in the corridor. "Me and Adams understand this sort of thing. Don't we?"

The Gunsmith turned to face him. "I understand, son."

"Parako!" Smith bellowed with rage.

Clint and Parako stood face to face, their legs splayed, pistols pointing at each other. The Gunsmith nodded and lowered his Colt. Parako responded likewise. Both men slid their guns into leather.

"Your move," Clint said, hoping he could dispatch Parako and turn to deal with Smith before the easterner could take advantage of the new circumstances.

Parako, however, presented the greater threat at that moment. Clint couldn't allow himself to take his attention off the young, lightning-fast pistolman. The Gunsmith also had to give Parako credit. The youth had guts, even if he was short on brains.

Parako made his move, his hand streaking for the gun on his hip. Clint's Colt fired before the younger man's weapon could clear its holster. The orange glare of the muzzle flash illuminated Parako's face, which had suddenly acquired a black hole between its eyes. Blood gushed from the cavity as Parako fell backward to the floor.

Clint instantly whirled to confront Baltimore Smith, realizing the easterner had already had ample time to attack. He was right. The Gunsmith saw brass studs flash as Smith's belt struck out at him like a deadly snake. Clint felt leather and metal smash into his hand, knocking the pistol from his grasp.

The light of the lantern on the floor cast a ghastly yellow hue across Baltimore Smith's face as he snarled and lashed out with the belt in his fist. Clint brought up his arms to protect his face just in time. The belt slammed into his forearms with the force of a club, staggering the Gunsmith.

Baltimore Smith was not only bigger than Clint, he was armed with a lethal, flexible weapon as well. The Gunsmith had his diminutive New Line Colt under his shirt, but Smith's slashing belt didn't allow him time to reach for the holdout gun. Clint had to act quickly before the easterner beat him to a pulp and smashed his skull as he had Timber Barton's.

The Gunsmith suddenly charged into Smith before the other man could swing the belt again. He crashed into the easterner's chest and heard Smith grunt with surprise as the wind was knocked out of him. The force of the lunge sent both men stumbling into the railing, and abruptly they toppled over it and fell to the landing below.

Clint found himself on top of Smith, whose body had absorbed the bulk of the impact from the fall, stunning the easterner. The Gunsmith immediately took advantage of this and punched Smith in the mouth as hard as he could.

The man from Baltimore responded by swinging his belt at Clint, but the weapon's efficiency was reduced in those close quarters. The blow hit Clint's left shoulder, jarring him slightly. Then Smith jabbed a left to Clint's jaw, knocking him backward.

The Gunsmith felt his footing slip. Then he was tumbling sideways down the stairs. Clint managed to relax his muscles enough to avoid a bone-breaking fall and came to rest at the next landing, bruised but uninjured.

He rose swiftly, about to reach for his belly gun, but Smith was already charging down the stairs after him, the belt swinging overhead in a vicious circle. Clint again launched himself forward, meeting the attack. His right shoulder rammed into Smith's abdomen as his arms scooped up his opponent's legs. Then Clint straightened his back and sent Baltimore Smith hurtling down the remaining flight of stairs.

Smith screamed before he hit the stairs. Unlike Clint, the Baltimore killer had fallen headfirst in a dead dive. His scream ended when he struck. His body continued down the stairs in an awkward somersault. Baltimore Smith reached the floor, his neck twisted in an ugly position.

Breathing hard and smarting from head to toe, Clint reached inside his shirt for the New Line Colt. Then he heard the triple click of a revolver hammer being cocked and stared up to see Alfred Jarrad standing on the landing above—pistol in hand, the muzzle aimed at the Gunsmith.

FORTY-ONE

"You should have stayed out of this, Adams," Jarrad declared. "Now your interference will cost you your life."

"No, Father!" Sylvia cried as she drifted to his side from the head of the stairs. "Hasn't there been enough killing?"

"Not quite," the rancher said in a hard, cold voice.

"You won't accomplish anything by killing me," Clint told him, his hands still inside his shirt, fingers touching the grips of the small .22 pistol hidden there. "It's over."

"It'll be over for *you* in another second or two, Adams," Jarrad replied calmly. "Just one question: Why?"

"Why did I join the miners at Jackass Gap?" The Gunsmith raised his eyebrows. "Because they're trying to earn their silver instead of taking it. Because they're not driven by bitter memories and unreasonable hatred. Because they're right and you're wrong, Jarrad."

"Well"—the rancher smiled thinly—"thank you for answering me. Now that we've settled that, I can kill you—"

Without warning, Sylvia seized Jarrad's arm and pulled forcibly, yanking the aim of the pistol away from Clint Adams. The rancher's finger jerked the trigger and a

176

muffled explosion filled the stairwell. The report of the
revolver had been muted because the muzzle had been
jammed against Sylvia's chest when Jarrad fired the gun.

Sylvia's body jerked from the impact of the bullet, yet
she stood and faced her father. Jarrad's features filled with
horror. His eyes bulged and his jaw hung open, his mouth
twisted downward by agony that penetrated his very soul.
Sylvia blinked in surprise, apparently feeling no pain
despite the fact a bullet had punched through her chest.
She displayed a weak smile. Graceful, even in death, she
folded into a neat pile at her father's feet.

"Sylvia-a-a!" Jarrad cried, falling to his knees beside
the girl's still form.

The Gunsmith had been stunned by what he had witnessed, yet he kept his wits and drew the New Line Colt
from his shirt. He watched Jarrad gather up his daughter's
corpse in his arms. The rancher buried his face in her
white-blond hair and wept.

"No-o-o!" Jarrad wailed. "She can't die! She's all I
have!"

"Didn't you realize that until now?" Clint asked.

Jarrad's tearstained face looked up. There was no anger
or hatred in his expression. His pride and majesty had
vanished with the life of his daughter. All that remained
was grief and defeat and the realization that he—and no
one else—had been responsible for the destruction of what
he'd loved most.

The Gunsmith saw Jarrad raise his pistol. He didn't try
to stop the rancher from putting the muzzle against the
side of his own head. He would later try to recall what he'd
felt as he watched Alfred W. Jarrad blow his brains out
right before his eyes. In truth, he felt nothing. Whatever
life had remained in the rancher had disappeared before he
squeezed the trigger. . . .

And a dead man can't really commit suicide.

FORTY-TWO

The final battle between the rancher's forces and the people of Jackass Gap had not been bloodless, yet Clint could only truly regret the death of one individual that night—Sylvia Jarrad. The shooting match at the bunkhouse had ended with two of the hired gunmen meeting an early, if predictable, death. None of the men in the Gunsmith's crew was killed or injured.

Clint was relieved and delighted to discover Carolyn Gray Fox had survived the ordeal without a scratch, although his own feelings for the girl both excited and terrified him. Love makes one vulnerable, and more often than not, it is a road to pain and disappointment rather than the joy and fulfillment written of in poetry. The Gunsmith wasn't certain he wanted to gamble with those stakes, Yet, can a man ignore or even control his heart in such matters?

First, however, Clint and his group had to see to the survivors of Jarrad's private army. At dawn, they transported twenty-three prisoners to Lodeville and explained the situation to a baffled and dumbfounded sheriff. The gunmen were placed under arrest and charged as accessories to murder and with conspiracy to commit murder and armed robbery. The federal marshals were contacted by telegram and agreed to send a team of lawmen to the

Great Basin to investigate the incident, and a circuit judge would be arriving for the trial later that month.

Clint wondered what would happen to Jarrad's property now. What would old George and the other servants do? Who would tend to the cattle and work the fields? It was a tragedy that Jarrad wasted his life, consumed by memories of what he'd lost instead of appreciating what he had.

While the Gunsmith and eight of the miners escorted their prisoners to Lodeville and saw to their incarceration and made certain the telegrams were sent to insure the gunmen would stand trial, Carolyn and two other miners returned to Jackass Gap to tell them of the success of the midnight assault. The nightmare was over and they could once again return to the mine and to digging their fortune from the Hill of Hope—which might eventually earn its name after all.

When Clint Adams and his eight companions returned to the mining town three days later, they could hardly recognize it. The somber atmosphere of a town under siege had vanished. Colored paper and cloth had been tied to clotheslines to form a row of pendants to welcome the Gunsmith's return. Harmonica and accordion music played gaily. Children played openly in the center of town. Clint was greeted not by hollow-featured sentries, but by the smiling faces of friends.

As he dismounted the Gunsmith thanked the cheering crowd that assembled around him to shake his hand and slap him on the back, searching for Carolyn's face among them. Ben hobbled forward on his crutch and warmly shook hands with the Gunsmith.

"You did it, Clint," he said. "There's no way we can ever thank you enough. . . ."

"That's okay, Ben," Clint assured him. "I don't see Carolyn."

"She's in her quarters—along with another surprise," Ben replied with a smile. Tears began to form in his eyes. "A wonderful surprise. Clint, I'm going to thank God every day for the rest of my life for what He's given me—and what He's given *back* to me."

The Gunsmith, totally confused by Ben's remarks, merely nodded and hurried to Carolyn's shack. He knocked on the door and a man's voice told him to enter. Startled, he opened the door to see Carolyn seated on a chair beside her bed, the same bed where she and Clint had first made love.

The bed was now occupied by a handsome young man with black hair and hazel eyes. He even had a crutch propped by the edge of the bed. No wonder. His right leg ended in a stump above the knee.

"Hello, Clint," Carolyn said, rising from her chair, a forced smile on her lovely face. "I'm glad you came back."

"Clint Adams!" the fellow on the bed exclaimed, struggling to sit up. "I've heard so much about you, I feel like we're old friends. Carolyn, Father, everybody has told me what you've done."

Clint stepped forward and shook hands with the one-legged man. "Then you must be Thomas Jefferson Watson."

"Just Tom." The fellow smiled. "You're probably surprised I'm alive. Even Dad and Carolyn thought Jarrad's men had killed me. Well, they nearly did. I was shot . . . pretty obvious where. Just like Dad, only I didn't get the bullet out in time. I don't know how long I lay there on the ground, half-conscious, sort of in a state of shock, I guess.

"Then along came some Mormons. One of them had been a doctor before he'd been driven out of Colorado because he's married to two women. He told me gangrene had set in so they had to amputate. He didn't explain that until *after* they'd cut off my leg because I was too feverish at the time to understand. Sure wish I'd realized what they were doing at the time it happened. Having a couple fellas tie you down and pull off your trousers while one of them has a knife in his hand is pretty scary.''

Clint looked at Carolyn, stunned by Tom's statement. "Yeah," he said softly. "Sounds like something out of a nightmare.''

FORTY-THREE

"You're leaving, Clint?" Carolyn Gray Fox inquired as she watched the Gunsmith tie Duke to the rear of his wagon.

"Ben and Tom paid me the three thousand in silver and everybody generously pitched in to restock my supplies," he replied. "Guess it's time to go." Clint turned to face her. "After all, I don't really have any reason to stay, do I?"

"Clint," she began, looking into his dark brown eyes with her remarkable green orbs misted by tears. "I don't know how much I feel for you, or how much I *could* feel for you if things were different."

"You loved Tom before you met me," the Gunsmith sighed. "And you still love him."

"Yes," Carolyn admitted. "And I love you too. I don't know which of you I love the most, but I can't leave Tom. He needs me, Clint. He needs me in every way now."

"Yeah." He nodded as he turned away.

"Clint," she said sharply. "Would you ask me to leave with you now? To leave Tom crippled for life and alone?"

The Gunsmith again faced her. "Of course not, Carolyn."

"So there really isn't any choice to make." She smiled. "Take care of yourself, darling."

Carolyn leaned forward and kissed him gently on the lips. Then she hurried back to her shack and to Tom Watson.

Clint Adams rode his wagon into the dry, barren prairie once again. He tried to mentally push the events of the past few days out of his mind. He decided to head for Carson City or maybe California, all the way to San Francisco. Spend some of his newly acquired wealth. Eat, drink, gamble, chase the ladies for a week or so and maybe he'd lose the emptiness and pain that lingered in his heart. Maybe . . .

"Hey, Clint!" a familiar female voice called.

He yanked back the reins of his team to stop the wagon and looked back at the one-horse carriage that galloped toward him. Darlene Farrell drove her buggy next to Clint's rig and brought it to a halt. She displayed a wide smile, and to his surprise Clint found himself responding to Darlene's charm as he vividly recalled her sexual prowess.

"You headed for Virginia City?" the beautiful journalist inquired.

"What's in Virginia City?" Clint asked with a grin.

"They've got a telegraph office for me, saloons for you and a hotel room for both of us," she replied brightly. "If you'd like some company."

"Still looking for material for your story?" Clint laughed.

"My story is finished and I'll be heading back East with it next week," Darlene shrugged. "But that still gives me a few days to celebrate my success . . . or *our* success, if you'd care to join me."

"Honey," the Gunsmith answered, "you've got yourself a deal."

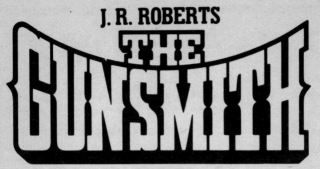

J. R. ROBERTS
THE GUNSMITH

SERIES

☐ 30856-2	THE GUNSMITH #1: MACKLIN'S WOMEN	$2.25
☐ 30857-0	THE GUNSMITH #2: THE CHINESE GUNMEN	$2.25
☐ 30858-9	THE GUNSMITH #3: THE WOMAN HUNT	$2.25
☐ 30859-7	THE GUNSMITH #4: THE GUNS OF ABILENE	$2.25
☐ 30860-0	THE GUNSMITH #5: THREE GUNS FOR GLORY	$2.25
☐ 30861-9	THE GUNSMITH #6: LEADTOWN	$2.25
☐ 30862-7	THE GUNSMITH #7: THE LONGHORN WAR	$2.25
☐ 30863-5	THE GUNSMITH #8: QUANAH'S REVENGE	$2.25
☐ 30864-3	THE GUNSMITH #9: HEAVYWEIGHT GUN	$2.25
☐ 30865-1	THE GUNSMITH #10: NEW ORLEANS FIRE	$2.25
☐ 30866-X	THE GUNSMITH #11: ONE-HANDED GUN	$2.25
☐ 30867-8	THE GUNSMITH #12: THE CANADIAN PAYROLL	$2.25
☐ 30868-6	THE GUNSMITH #13: DRAW TO AN INSIDE DEATH	$2.25
☐ 30869-4	THE GUNSMITH #14: DEAD MAN'S HAND	$2.25
☐ 30872-4	THE GUNSMITH #15: BANDIT GOLD	$2.25
☐ 30886-4	THE GUNSMITH #16: BUCKSKINS AND SIX-GUNS	$2.25

Available at your local bookstore or return this form to:

 CHARTER BOOKS
Book Mailing Service
P.O. Box 690, Rockville Centre, NY 11571

Please send me the titles checked above. I enclose _____ include $1.00 for postage and handling if one book is ordered; 50¢ per book for two or more. California, Illinois, New York and Tennessee residents please add sales tax.

NAME _____

ADDRESS _____

CITY _____ STATE/ZIP _____

(allow six weeks for delivery)

A1

Bestselling Books

- [ ] 16663-3 **DRAGON STAR** Olivia O'Neill $2.95
- [ ] 46895-0 **LADY JADE** Leslie O'Grady $3.25
- [ ] 55258-7 **THE MYRMIDON PROJECT** Chuck Scarborough & William Murray $3.25
- [ ] 65366-9 **THE PATRIARCH** Chaim Bermant $3.25
- [ ] 70885-4 **REBEL IN HIS ARMS** Francine Rivers $3.50
- [ ] 78374-0 **STAR STRUCK** Linda Palmer $3.25
- [ ] 02572-2 **APOCALYPSE BRIGADE** Alfred Coppel $3.50
- [ ] 65219-0 **PASSAGE TO GLORY** Robin Leigh Smith $3.50
- [ ] 75887-8 **SENSEI** David Charney $3.50
- [ ] 05285-1 **BED REST** Rita Kashner $3.25
- [ ] 62674-2 **ON ANY GIVEN SUNDAY** Ben Elisco $3.25
- [ ] 09233-0 **CASHING IN** Antonia Gowar $3.50
- [ ] 75700-6 **SEASON OF THE STRANGLER** Madison Jones $2.95

Available at your local bookstore or return this form to:

 CHARTER BOOKS
Book Mailing Service
P.O. Box 690, Rockville Centre, NY 11571

Please send me the titles checked above. I enclose _____.
Include $1.00 for postage and handling if one book is ordered; 50¢ per book for two or more. California, Illinois, New York and Tennessee residents please add sales tax.

NAME _____

ADDRESS _____

CITY _____ STATE/ZIP _____

(allow six weeks for delivery)   A-4